STAR WARS®
DARK FORCES™

Jedi Knight

Also Available
Star Wars: Dark Forces — Soldier for the Empire
by William C. Dietz & Dean Williams

Star Wars: Dark Forces — Rebel Agent
by William C. Dietz & Ezra Tucker

STAR WARS®
DARK FORCES™
Jedi Knight

Written by
WILLIAM C. DIETZ

Illustrated by
DAVE DORMAN

A DARK HORSE COMICS®
& BOULEVARD/PUTNAM BOOK

Dark Horse Comics, Inc.
Publisher Mike Richardson
10956 SE Main Street
Milwaukie, OR 97222

G. P. Putnam's Sons
Publishers Since 1838
A member of Penguin Putnam Inc.
375 Hudson Street
New York, NY 10014

Editors
SUZANNE TAYLOR
CHRIS WARNER
GINJER BUCHANAN
& ALLAN KAUSCH

Jacket and book designers
JULIE GASSAWAY
BRIAN GOGOLIN
& CARY GRAZZINI

Special thanks to
ARTHUR BAKER

This trilogy of graphic story albums is based on the characters and
situations from LucasArts' DARK FORCES and JEDI KNIGHT games and
would not have been possible without the invaluable assistance of Justin
Chin and the development staff of LucasArts Entertainment Company.

This is book three of a trilogy of titles:
*Star Wars®: Dark Forces™ — Soldier for the Empire,
Rebel Agent*, and *Jedi Knight*.

Library of Congress Cataloging-in-Publication Data

Dietz, William C.
Star Wars: dark forces, jedi knight/ by William C. Dietz.
p. cm.
Sequel to: Star Wars: dark forces, rebel agent
ISBN: 0-399-14452-8 (alk. paper)
I. Dorman, Dave. II. Title.
PN6727.D54D37 1998   98-22691
CIP
741.5'973—dc21

Printed in the United States of America
1 3 5 7 9 10 8 6 4 2

To Marjorie,
who climbed the mountain,
took the wrong train,
swam the river,
lived in the hotel,
did things that scared her,
gave birth to daughters,
taught children how to think,
roamed the world,
let me go, held me close,
listened to my dreams
and made them come true.

My thanks to Dave Dorman for the art that graces
this book, to Justin Chin and the development staff of
LucasArts Entertainment Company that created DARK FORCES,
to the eternally helpful Lucy Autrey Wilson, Allan Kausch,
David Scroggy, Lynn Adair, Ginjer Buchanan, and last,
but certainly not least, to George Lucas and the
other minds who created this universe.
May the Force be with you.

BILL DIETZ

To St. George.

My thanks to Phil Burnett, Lurene Haines, Jack Petry,
Kris Lagerloef, and Jenny Prestwood for their assistance
in modeling; to Justin Chin (a lifesaver for reference) and
William Dietz for great source material; to Gary Newman for
the Moldy Crow; to Dark Horse, David Scroggy, Lynn Adair,
Suzanne Taylor, and especially Mike Richardson, who put his
trust in me; to my Lucasfilm family, including Allan Kausch,
Lucy Autrey Wilson, and of course George Lucas;
and to Star Wars fans around the world.

DAVE DORMAN

Jedi Knight

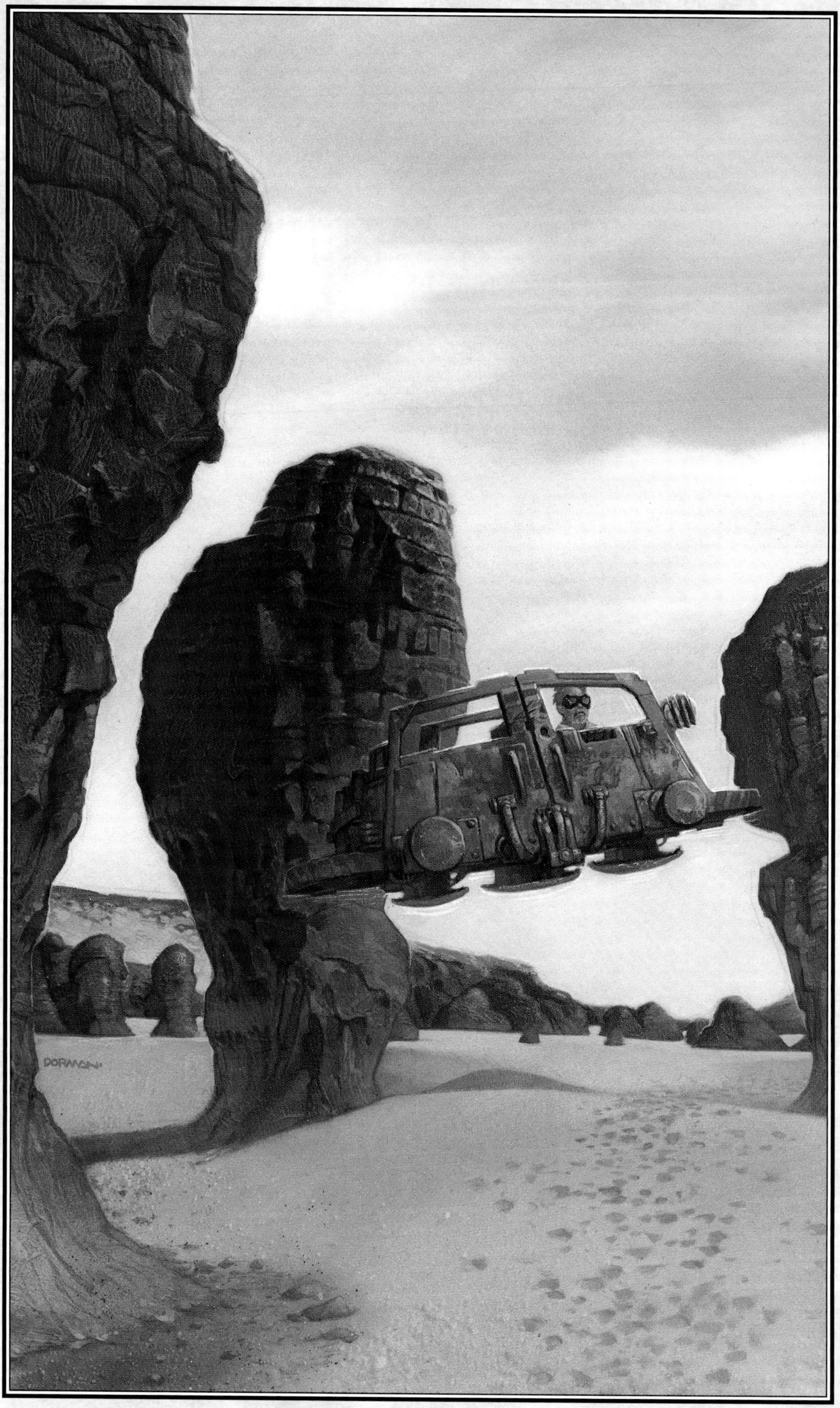
DORMAN

CHAPTER 1

The airspeeder, a world-weary affair built from salvage and held together by incessant prayer, coughed, sputtered, and lurched through the air. It had been yellow once, but that was long ago, and large islands of rust dotted the sun-bleached paint. An outcropping of rock rose ahead.

The machine's sole occupant had a two-day growth of beard and eyes that peered from skin-draped caves. He saw the danger, swore, and fiddled with the controls. The repulsorlift engine cut out, caught, and pushed the machine higher. The top-most spire passed within a meter of the speeder's belly. The vehicle sagged as if exhausted by the effort, and Grif Grawley patted the console. "Thata girl . . . you done good . . . real good."

The settler peered over the side — saw the airspeeder's shadow flit across the land — and watched his gra bounce along the flats below. He knew where they were headed. The wind-sculpted hill, one of many left to mark the retreat of an ancient glacier, had triggered one of their preprogrammed instincts: "Look for the high ground when the light starts to fade — and watch for predators."

A survival strategy that *seemed* natural — but was actually the result of extensive genetic engineering. Genetic engineering that had proven so reliable that gra sperm and ova were normally sold "by the herd" and came with an electronic manual. A manual that Grif had memorized during the long trip to Ruusan.

A pile of boulders appeared in their path, and the herd split into two groups, one that followed Alpha, the dominant male, and one that trailed Beta, his mate.

The hill was closer now, and Grif dumped speed. The speeder was fragile, *very* fragile, and the settler didn't fancy a fifty-kilometer walk to Fort Nowhere, the *only* human outpost on Ruusan.

The speeder slowed, hovered over the summit, and settled onto skid marks left from previous landings. Grif cut power, ran the check list, and secured the tie-downs. The wind came up at night — and it paid to be careful.

Then, with the surety of someone who has done something a hundred times, Grif set up camp. The shelter opened and locked with authoritative "snap." The combination cook chest and food locker extended its legs and stood beside the tent.

That's when Grif opened a much-abused metal case. Components, each hand crafted from whatever Grif could beg, borrow, or steal lay snuggled within.

He removed the assemblies one by one, held them up to the quickly fading light, and blew imaginary grit from their workings. Each unit made a satisfying "click" as it mated with the next. The object, which Grif called "Fido," was shaped like a boomerang and equipped with an assortment of sensors. The miniature flyer was designed to stay aloft all night, watch for signs of danger, and alert Grif should any appear. The machine beeped as it came to life and shivered while its gyro spun up.

The settler checked the machine's readouts, assured himself that all systems were green, and threw the device off a nearby cliff. Fido propelled itself into a thermal, switched its power plant to standby, and soared into the quickly darkening sky.

Grif checked a monitor, verified the quality of the incoming holos, and returned to his chores. The gra were halfway up the hill by then, picking their way through the scree, and nibbling on tough, rubbery plants. A series of cliffs would hold them at that level until morning came.

Half an hour later, with a tumbler of what the locals referred to as "Old Trusty" to keep him company and a fabulous view of the setting sun, Grif called his wife.

Carole Grawley was expecting the call and smiled as she lifted the handset. "Grif?"

"Hi, honey . . . I'm sitting on top of hill 461 . . . and everything's fine."

Carole carried the comm set out onto the flat piece of hard-packed dirt they jokingly called "the veranda." The house, which had been dug into a hillside twenty klicks south of Fort Nowhere, faced south to take advantage of the winter sun. Hill 461 was southwest of her position, and Carole looked in that direction. "How's the sunset? It looks marvelous from here."

Grif pictured his wife's face, still beautiful in spite of the heavily ridged scar tissue, and smiled. "It's gorgeous, honey . . . just like you."

Carole Grawley smiled, knew he meant it, and changed the subject. "The pump's acting up again. I have drinking water, and enough for the garden, but the irrigation system is dry. The crops have started to droop."

Grif thought about the fact that the cave farmers had all the water they could use and wondered if they were right. "Outcropping," which was the name they used to describe what he and his wife did, was much more difficult than it had been on Sulon. Of course, working down in a cave, using light piped in from the surface, had its drawbacks, too. Like being closed in. Grif took a pull from his drink. "No problem, honey. I'll fix ol' Jenny soon as I get back."

Carole Grawley smiled at her husband's propensity for naming machinery and watched the sun disappear beyond the western horizon. "I know you will, Grif — take care of yourself out there."

"You can count on it," Grif replied. "Be sure to set the perimeter alarms. I'll call tomorrow."

"Love you . . . "

"Love you, too — good night."

With no sun to warm it, the air cooled quickly. Grif was able to see his breath by the time dinner was over and the first of Ruusan's three satellites popped over the Eastern horizon. The smugglers who built Fort Nowhere referred to the moons as "the triplets" and swore there were ruins on one of them. Not that it made much difference to Grif. He had other things to worry about.

The settler tossed back his drink, poured himself another, and checked Fido's scanner readings. The flyer, which circled the hill at regular five-minute intervals, assured him that everything was under control.

All 136 of the gra were accounted for, no predators had infiltrated the area, and atmospheric conditions were normal.

In fact, the only anomaly, assuming it qualified as such, was that the planet's network of sixteen combination weather and surveillance satellites had gone off the air. Not unheard of, but unusual, especially in light of the fact that the smugglers who had placed the machines in orbit were fanatical about maintenance. Still, things can and do go wrong, and Grif assumed that the problem would be identified and subsequently fixed.

The third moon had risen by that time and, with help from its siblings, threw a soft white cloak across the land. Grif finished the second drink, considered a third, and knew Carole would disapprove.

That being the case, he removed the electrobinoculars from their place in the skimmer and walked to the highest point on the hill. There was very little chance that he would spot the elusive natives, bouncing and floating across the land, but he never stopped trying. What some of his fellow settlers regarded with fear and loathing, he considered beautiful and fascinating.

Grif switched the electrobinoculars to infrared, chose a spot on the southern horizon, and quartered the area.

Rocks, still warm from the sun, glowed green in the viewfinder. Light streaked across the screen as a bush runner dashed from one location to another. He moved the glasses farther to the right — and that's when he saw the bouncer's telltale shape. It was round, like a ball. The settler felt his pulse pound as he pressed the zoom control. The image grew larger.

But wait, something was wrong, *very* wrong. The heat signature was too large, too intense, and too high in the air.

Grif knew how much the indigs loved to roll in front of the wind, bounce into the air, and float until gravity pulled them down. They got fifty or sixty meters' worth of altitude off a good bounce sometimes, but this object was a good deal higher than that.

So what could it be? Whatever it was had the capacity to hover — and move *against the prevailing wind*. Grif watched the glowing, green globe grow larger, realized it was coming his way, and felt the bottom drop out of his stomach. Since he could see *it* . . . it could see him!

Memories flickered through his mind, memories of an Imperial probe droid that drifted through the mist, memories of energy beams that stabbed the walls of his home, and the knowledge that he had no way to stop them.

He remembered the explosion, the flames, and the sound of Katie's screams. He remembered how Carole had tried to enter the house, how he had pulled her out, and how the structure had collapsed a few seconds later.

Carole had been on fire by then, screaming her daughter's name, kicking and biting as he pulled her away. All because the family had taken part in a brave but futile protest against the Imperial presence on Sulon. A Rebel leader named Morgan Katarn had spirited them away — and brought them to Ruusan — but there was no escaping the memories.

Grif watched the image grow and knew it had locked on to the heat radiating off the airspeeder. The only question was whether the droid had been launched by an Imperial vessel on its way through the system — or by a ship in orbit. The first theory was consistent with the way Imperial scout ships were known to operate, while the second would explain why the weather satellites had gone off the air.

Not that it made a whole lot of difference, since the course of action would be the same. Destroy the probe, warn the others, and hope for the best. It was all that Grif or anyone else could do.

The settler's heart pounded against his chest as he ran downhill, skidded to a stop, and used his hunting knife to sever the tie-downs. The speeder creaked as he climbed aboard.

Work-thickened fingers stabbed at the controls, rows of lights appeared, and the repulsorlift engine whined into life. The machine rocked slightly as it came off the ground, faltered as energy tried to arc across two badly worn contacts, and steadied as Grif babied the controls.

Then, with Fido still circling above, the settler took off. He stood up in order to improve his visibility and felt the wind press against his face. Moonlight gleamed off the droid's highly polished skin. He aimed for the reflection and wished he had a plan.

"When in doubt, improvise," Grif mumbled to himself, grabbed the blast rifle racked along the port side, and removed the safety. A green "ready" light appeared as he rested the barrel on the top of the windshield and squeezed the trigger.

The energy pulse blipped outward, missed the probe by a good twenty meters, and disappeared. Grif corrected his aim, fired again, and saw the bolt hit. The blast slagged one of the droid's sensors, took the shine off a few square centimeters of alloy skin, and triggered a preprogrammed response.

The probe came equipped with four energy cannons, one for each point of the compass, and brought one of them to bear. The right side of the windshield disappeared as the energy beam slashed through it.

Grif swore, put the speeder into the tightest turn he could, and saw another beam pass through the air just vacated. The fight, if that's what it could properly be called, was anything but fair. What he needed was a way to even the odds.

The settler pushed the speeder down toward the surface. The lower he went, the more energy could be converted into forward momentum. The fact that the droid would be forced to convert more of its onboard computing capacity to low-level navigation amounted to a bonus.

Grif knew the territory ahead — and knew the ground would rise. A ridge appeared, and he aimed for the V-shaped gap at the top. Energy strobed past, struck an outcropping, and sliced it off. The speeder passed through, banked to the right, and hugged the south side of the ridge.

The droid burst through the gap, lost the flyer's heat signature in the warmth radiating off the rock, and switched to holo cams.

Grif brought the speeder to a momentary halt, pulled the remote free of the control panel, and grabbed the blast rifle. Then, praying there was enough time, the settler vaulted over the side.

His knees bent to absorb the shock, the rifle clattered as it hit the ground, and the remote filled his fist. He thumbed the "on" button, moved the slider forward, and watched the machine accelerate away. The probe altered course and fired. The bolt missed. So far, so good. Now for the second and most crucial part of the plan . . .

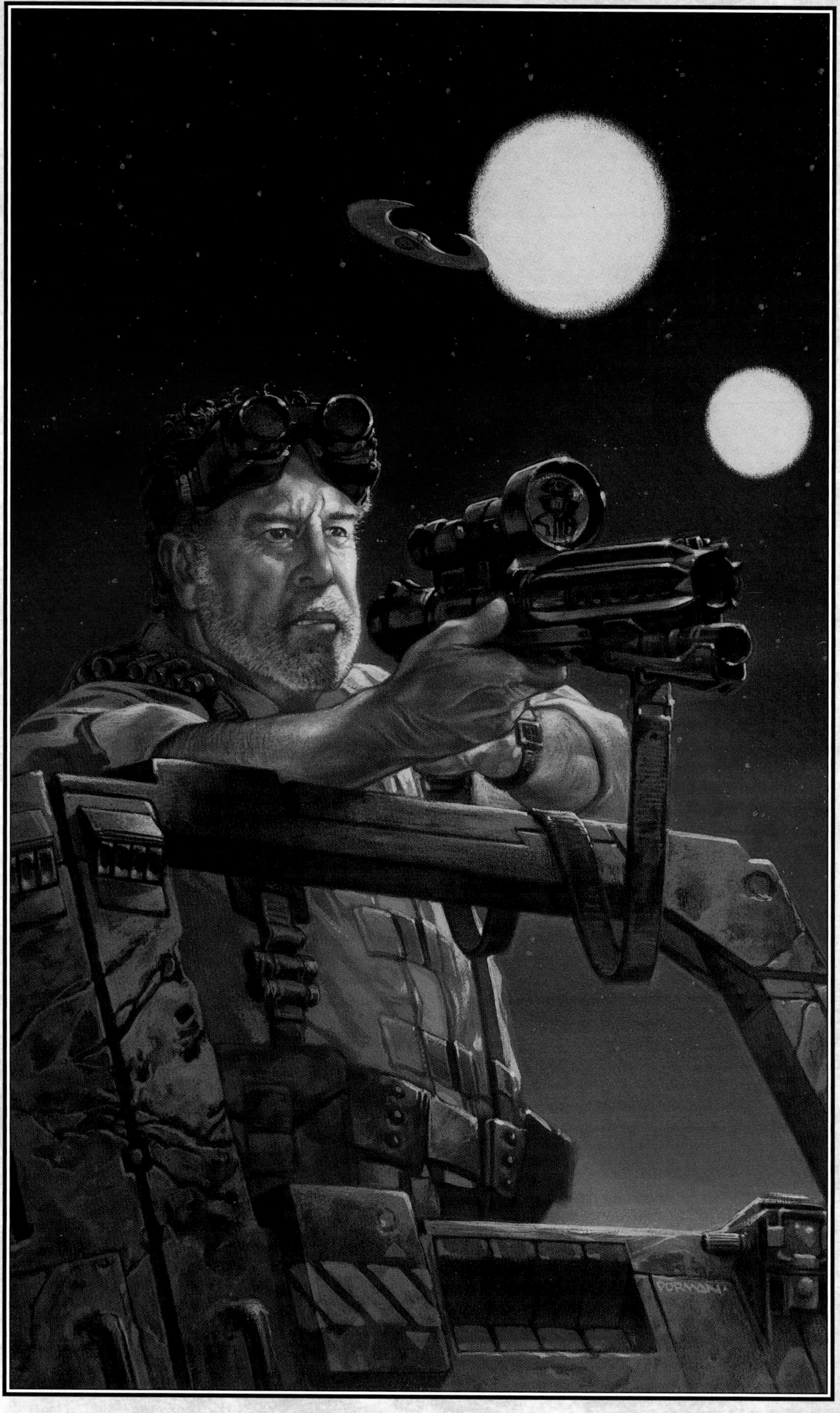

Grif turned the directional knob to the right, waited for the airspeeder to respond accordingly, and swore when it didn't. As with so much of his homegrown equipment, the remote had a tendency to malfunction. He tried again with similar results.

The probe fired, the flyer staggered under the impact of a direct hit, and Grif turned the directional knob to the left. It worked this time, the next bolt missed, and the machine trailed smoke.

The settler gritted his teeth, twisted the control as far as it would go, and watched the speeder turn on its attacker. The droid fired, slagged what remained of the windshield, and prepared to finish what it had started.

The speeder completed its turn. Grif centered the directional control, gave thanks when the vehicle lurched onto the correct path, and pushed the slider to max. "Sorry, old girl, but there's no other way."

The airspeeder picked up speed, fell as the engine slipped out of phase, and struggled to rise. The probe fired, missed, and triggered a targeting laser.

Grif stood, *willed* the speeder to endure another five seconds of punishment, and cheered as it bored in. "That'a baby! You can do it!"

The droid fired and was still in the process of firing when the speeder hit, and both machines exploded. A reddish-orange flower blossomed; sent long, fiery tendrils up into the sky; and was snuffed from existence.

Grif watched the debris tumble toward the ground and felt momentary elation quickly followed by despair. The Imperials had found Ruusan, and the dream was over. Nothing would be the same again. Life, difficult though it had been, was about to get worse.

The settler considered his options. The smugglers had designed Fort Nowhere to withstand a force-one raid. Assuming the probe had been dropped into the planet's atmosphere by a passing ship, or belonged to a lightly armed scout, they still had a chance. *If* he could warn them. *If* they would listen. *If* they took action.

His transportation was spread all over the countryside, and Fort Nowhere was approximately fifty kilometers away. Which strategy should he pursue? Hoof it? Or return to the hill?

The comm set would be where he'd left it, sitting on top of the food locker. But what about the climb? What if he fell? A distinct possibility given the lack of climbing equipment.

Grif sighed, hoped Alpha would keep the herd together, and grabbed the blast rifle. It made a comforting weight. He turned toward the north and started to walk. He had a long way to go and nothing better to do.

The compartment, which was the largest the *Vengeance* had to offer, was almost painfully Spartan. No shelves, no pictures, and no keepsakes. Nothing but a standard bunk, a custom easy chair, and a crystal-clear bowl filled with multicolored touchstones.

Some among the few privileged enough to enter the compartment assumed that the lack of ornamentation stemmed from the fact that Jerec was blind and presumably uninterested in that which he couldn't see. They were wrong.

Others believed that the Spartan conditions were the result of the severe discipline that the Jedi imposed on himself. They were wrong as well.

The truth, like the man to whom it pertained, was more complicated than that. Material things meant nothing to Jerec — not unless they added to his power — for to have power is to have physical objects when and where you want them.

Jerec settled into his chair, felt it adjust to his body, and allowed Borna's second symphony to flow over and around him. The composer had been a Rebel — and the dark, moody music the Jedi enjoyed so much had been a protest against the Imperial government. It was too bad that Borna had died so young, but art and politics make poor bedfellows.

Jerec smiled and allowed his fingers to enter the bowl. The touchstones came in a variety of shapes, sizes, and textures. Some were smooth and cool to the touch, while others were coarse and warmed from within.

The Jedi selected what felt like a star, positioned it under his nose, and popped the casing. The scent of wild flowers entered his nostrils, formed a counterpoint to the music, and carried him away. He imagined the future, the throne upon which he would sit, and the power he would wield. All because of the planet below — and the secret hidden there.

The knock was so soft that Jerec could have ignored it had he chosen to do so. But he knew who it was and wanted to hear her report. "Enter."

Sariss was young, beautiful, and dressed in black. Her blood-red lips, nails, and collar made the black seem blacker. She entered the compartment, allowed the hatch to close, and waited for Jerec to speak. He ran his fingers through the stones, found a triangle, and offered it up. "For you, my dear."

Sariss viewed the tidbit with both annoyance and suspicion. It was his way of maintaining his power over her. A game to be played. Should she eat it? Pop and sniff? She could ask Jerec, and symbolically reaffirm his superiority, or take her chances. The Jedi had tried that once before. She remembered the way the casing had split open, the stench that had filled the air, and Boc's laughter. It had been a thoroughly unpleasant and humiliating experience.

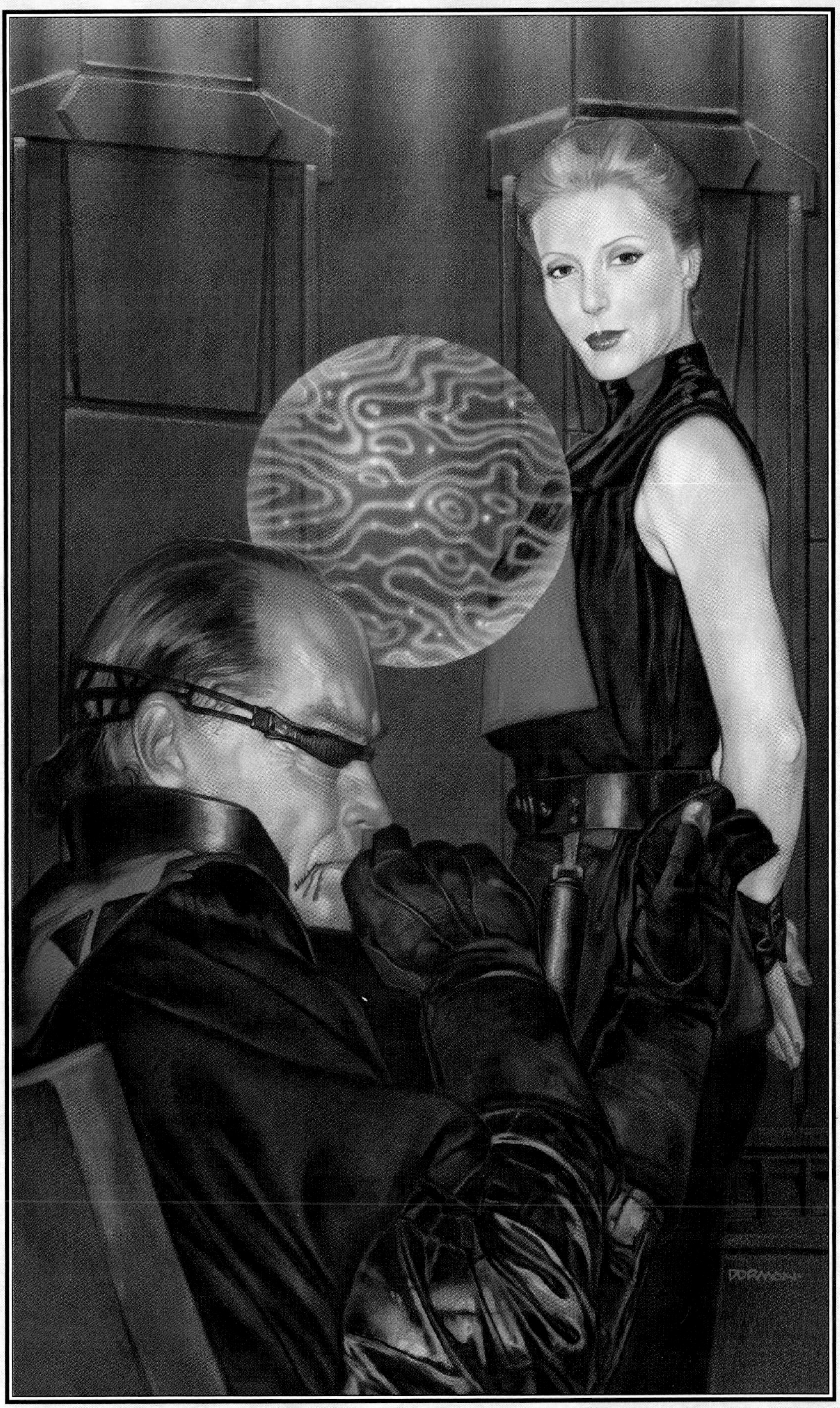
DORMAN

Jerec, who could imagine her dilemma, smiled. "What? You would refuse my gift?"

Sariss steeled herself, plucked the stone from his fingers, and popped it into her mouth. "Not at all . . . thank you for the treat."

The stone dissolved, vanilla-flavored syrup flooded her mouth, and Jerec chuckled. "Very good! I'm impressed! Now, tell me what you learned."

Sariss had a mind like a steel trap. She reeled off the facts from memory. "Phase one of the survey is complete. Phase two is underway."

Sariss produced a handheld holo projector and pressed a button. A likeness of Ruusan filled the center of the room. Jerec couldn't see it — but liked subordinates to pretend that he could. It made the Jedi seem omniscient, which added to the mystique associated with his name. The image started to rotate, and Sariss used it to focus her thoughts.

"Both the atmosphere and gravity are well within Class Three parameters. Surface mapping is 93.4 percent complete. Surface and subsurface scans reveal significant mineral deposits, including iron, copper, cesium, iridium, nickel, uranium, and a good many more. Of equal interest are seven already-exploited mines, all thousands of years old, none in production."

"Are they in or near the target area?"

"No, my lord. In spite of the fact that the subsurface probes confirm an extensive system of caves within the confines of the valley, they are not associated with significant mineral deposits. And while the facilities required to process ore might have disappeared over the millennia, the probes found no sign of tailings."

Jerec nodded. "Continue."

"The planet supports two cultures — the first consists of approximately 20,000 preindustrial sentients. They seem to be indigenous, although surface artifacts suggest that other species lived here as well, raising the possibility that they originated somewhere else."

"Yes," Jerec agreed. "The legends speak of many species — and a rich civilization. Tell me more about the humans."

Sariss shrugged. "There isn't much to tell . . . Space trash mostly, mixed with dissidents. The probes kept their distance but were able to monitor and record their comm traffic. Content analysis, combined with call mapping, confirms that most of the humans live and work in the vicinity of a Class Two military installation."

Jerec's eyebrows shot upward. "A military installation?"

"Yes, my lord. It appears that a gang of smugglers uses Ruusan to warehouse their contraband and built the fort to protect their property. They call it 'Fort Nowhere.' A rather apt name, all things considered. Our forces will attack tomorrow."

"No," Jerec said firmly, "they won't. Not without a visit. Take Yun and Boc. See what you can learn. Report to me."

The fact that Jerec had seen fit to countermand her plans brought blood to Sariss' face. His approval meant a great deal to her, and she worked hard to maintain it. Making a bad situation even worse was the fact that she disagreed with his orders. She cleared her throat. "May I ask why, my lord? Wouldn't such a visit put them on alert? And cause additional casualties among our troops?"

Jerec allowed himself a frown. "You doubt our ability to win?"

"No, my lord. Of course not."

"Good. There are reasons for my orders even when they aren't apparent to you. These people have lived on the planet for some time. Are they aware of the Valley? And if they are, did they loot the chambers? And if they did, what happened to the materials found there?"

They were intelligent questions, and the fact that she had failed to consider them brought even more blood to the Jedi's cheeks. She bowed, assured Jerec that his orders would be implemented, and backed out into the corridor.

Jerec waited until his subordinate had left, allowed his fingers to trail through the touchstones, and found a treat. It was shaped like Ruusan and cool to the touch. He brought it to his lips, popped the sphere into his mouth, and broke the outer skin. The liqueur tasted of cinnamon and contained a mild intoxicant. He smiled, thought about the embarrassment Sariss had experienced, and laughed out loud.

Grif was tired, *very* tired. He was in better shape than most men his age — no, *half* his age — but fifty kilometers is a long way to go. The sun had both risen and set since the battle with the droid.

He paused, took a moment to check his back trail, and produced a self-satisfied grunt. The sky was clear, the triplets were up, and there was nothing to be seen. No droids, skimmers, or speeder bikes rushing to catch up with him. Perhaps the probe *had* been on its own. He certainly hoped so.

Mountains had forced the settler toward the west. Assuming he was right, and this was the reverse slope of "Katarn's Hill," he was almost there.

Gravel slid out from under the colonist's boots. He swore, resisted the temptation to use the blast rifle as a walking stick, and fought his way upward.

The stench of a garbage-filled ravine confirmed his skill as a navigator. Grif wrinkled his nose, hurried to put the odor behind him, and crested the hill.

The homes, many of which had been sited with help from Morgan Katarn, were more than half buried in the soil, a strategy that helped them stay cool during the day and warm at night.

A scattering of yellow-orange rectangles marked the location of windows and hinted at the hospitality that waited within. Grif passed them by. It was evening, and that meant the majority of the colony's elected and unelected leaders would be gathered within the Smuggler's Rest, drinks in hand.

Grif licked his lips at the thought, ignored the half-tamed bush runner that lunged at the end of its chain, and followed the well-worn path toward the fort. He heard a snatch of conversation, the slamming of a door, and the whine of a multi-tool. Common sounds that he found comforting.

Fort Nowhere was laid out in the shape of a six-pointed star. Blaster cannons had been mounted at each of the star's points — a strategy that would place attackers in a withering crossfire.

The cannons, plus hidden missile batteries, were a potent threat against anything short of an Imperial assault, the very thing he had come to warn them about.

A voice called out from the shadows and asked, "Who goes there?" in a voice that didn't seem to care.

The settler paused. "Grif Grawley."

The sentry, a smuggler named Horley, stepped out into the moonlight. "Grif? Carole called. She's worried sick."

"I'll get back to her," Grif promised. "Soon as I can. Where's the fat guy who thinks he's mayor?"

Horley chuckled. "Same as always, sitting around the Rest, complaining about the Empire."

"Good. Keep a sharp eye out — or there might be even more to complain about."

The sentry wanted to ask what the comment meant, but Grawley was gone. Horley shivered, blamed the cool night breeze, and turned toward the badlands. Clouds claimed the triplets, and darkness obscured the land.

Grif heard the Smuggler's Rest before he actually saw it. The music, popular on Corellia two years before, was punctuated by laughter and the bong of the drink gong. Someone had bought a round.

Grif rounded a corner, nodded to a passing spacer, and strode the width of the inner courtyard. The all-too-familiar doors swung open at the touch of his hand, and he blinked in the sudden light. The bar had been crafted from a damaged fuel tank and lined one side of the room. A dozen mismatched tables made islands on the seldom-swept floor. The walls, which were covered with an unplanned montage of memorabilia, had launched many a story. There were fifteen or twenty people present. They turned as he entered the room.

"Look!" someone exclaimed. "It's Grif Grawley! Hey, Grif! Carole's looking for volunteers. Ya ain't gettin' any lighter, ya know!"

There was a chorus of guffaws as regulars had a laugh at Grif's expense. They remembered the night six months before, on the eve of little Katie's birthday, when Grif had attempted to anesthetize himself with an entire bottle of Old Trusty. Carole had been summoned and, with help from the regulars, had loaded him onto a skimmer. Anger flared — anger and resentment.

Grif swiveled toward his right, fired from the hip, and watched the sound system explode. Silence settled over the bar — interrupted only by the drip, drip, drip of liquefied components and the cooler's monotonous hum. Mayor Devo, his paunch hanging over his belt, was the first to recover. He came to his feet. A stubby index finger stabbed the air.

"And that will be enough of that! We've had enough from you, Grif Grawley. Place the weapon on the floor and take three steps backward."

The settler made no effort to obey. He reached under his jacket, found the flat piece of metal, and pulled it free of his waistband. It clanged as it hit the table.

Devo looked down and up again. He frowned. "And what's this supposed to be?"

"An ID plate. Read it."

Reluctantly, his face flushed with anger, the mayor did as he was told. The words seemed to echo through the bar. "Imperial Probe Droid PD 4786. So? What's your point?"

Grif allowed his eyes to roam the room. "So, I tangled with an Imperial probe droid, rammed it with my airspeeder, and hoofed it here. It could have been a loner, dumped into our atmosphere by a passing ship, or it could be part of something a lot worse. I suggest you pack what you can, load your families on skimmers, and follow me. There are places where you can hide."

There was silence for a moment followed by complete pandemonium. It seemed as if everyone had something to say.

"Throw the idiot out!"

"What if he's right? How did they find us?"

"I told you this would happen . . ."

"Grif wouldn't know a probe droid if it was floating in his whiskey . . ."

Grif tapped the gong with a half-empty bottle of Old Trusty. The babble ceased. Grif scanned the faces before him. "Believe what you want. One question, though. How do you explain the fact that the weather sats are down? Not just one of them . . . but the whole bunch?"

The settler turned toward a woman named Peeno. She was Captain Jerg's second in command — and some said more than that. "How 'bout it, Marie? You got those sats up and running yet?"

The smuggler, a woman with short red hair and a nose stud, shook her head. "They all went down about the same time. We've been unable to contact them since."

Grif persisted. "How 'bout ships? Got any in orbit?"

Jerg had left more than thirty days before and had taken the shuttles with him. Everyone knew he was gone, and everyone knew it would be another month before he returned. Peeno shook her head again.

Grif nodded. "Just as I thought. Heads in the sand — butts in the air. Good luck, 'cause you're gonna need it."

So saying, the settler took a long, hard pull from the bottle in his hand, slammed it down, and tossed a coin onto the bar. It spun, fell, and landed heads-up.

Grif was halfway across the courtyard by the time the yelling started — and only twenty klicks from home. It would be good to see Carole.

The sun had been up for some time when the Imperial assault shuttle approached from the south. It made a series of circles, each smaller than the last, as if those on board were sightseeing, which in a sense they were.

Sariss released her safety harness, stepped into the cockpit, and peered over the pilots' heads. Fort Nowhere shimmered in the heat. "What a dump."

Yun, a young, almost-boyish Jedi with a shock of brown hair, moved to join her. Partly because he was curious — and partly because she was his mentor. "That's for sure. I don't know what they ran away from, but it must have been pretty bad."

"It *was* pretty bad," Boc agreed, as he took up a position behind them. "They were running from us."

Peeno's head tracked the shuttle in concert with the fort's energy cannon. She wore a headset, torso armor, and carried her blast rifle on a sling. The number-three gunner, a colonist named Dinko, wanted to fire. "I can take her, lieutenant! Just say the word."

The shuttle turned, and Peeno turned with it. "Not a good idea, Dinko. That assault boat didn't come here all by herself. There's at least one ship, maybe more, in orbit above. If they wanted to grease us, they would have done it by now. Take your weapon off-line . . . and that goes for the rest of you, too. They want to talk, so let's give them the chance."

The shuttle flared, gave the colonists a peek at the registration numbers painted on its belly, and settled onto the pad. Grit sprayed sideways, and the noise brought even more of Fort Nowhere's citizens to the scene.

The settlers had expected stormtroopers, followed by an officer, but were in for a surprise. Eyes widened and mouths dropped as Sariss, Yun, and Boc exited the ship.

"Who are they?"

"They have lightsabers!"

"What's a worm-head doing here?"

"What's wrong with you people? Shoot them!"

The last comment came from a settler named Lasko. His first wife had given her life in defense of the Sulon G-Tap. The very sight of the Imperials filled him with hate.

The intensity of his emotions sent ripples through the Force. Sariss stopped, turned, and picked Lasko out of the crowd. The colonist looked surprised, brought his hands up to his throat, and struggled to breathe. His face turned blue, his knees buckled, and he thumped to the ground. Then, just as the life force started to leak out of his body, Sariss relented.

Lasko sucked air into his aching lungs, rubbed his throat, and stood. His friends and neighbors averted their eyes as the settler shouldered his way through the crowd. Then, having put the throng behind him, Lasko broke into a run. He had a new wife now and a six-month-old baby. He'd load the skimmer, head out into the badlands, and hope for the best.

Sariss took pleasure in the fear that surrounded her. Thanks to the settler, and his big mouth, a lesson had been learned. Resist, and you will die.

The crowd started to back away, to disperse, but Yun shook his head. "What's the hurry? Stick around — you'll stay healthy that way."

Boc started to laugh, a high-pitched gibbering sound that brought fear to the settlers' faces. Sariss stood with hands on hips. "So, who's in charge?"

There was silence, followed by sidelong glances and the shuffling of feet. That's when Mayor Devo was nudged, shouldered, and pushed out into the open. Once exposed, the politician tried to make the best of a bad situation. He adjusted his paunch, found a smile, and took three steps forward. "That would be me . . . Mayor Byron Devo III at your service. And you are?"

"My name is unimportant," Sariss replied coldly. "The important thing is that you, and your treasonous constituents, have established an illegal settlement for the purposes of smuggling and tax evasion. Both punishable by death."

Devo swallowed, realized that his hands had gone to his throat, and forced them down. It seemed as if the woman knew everything. Still,

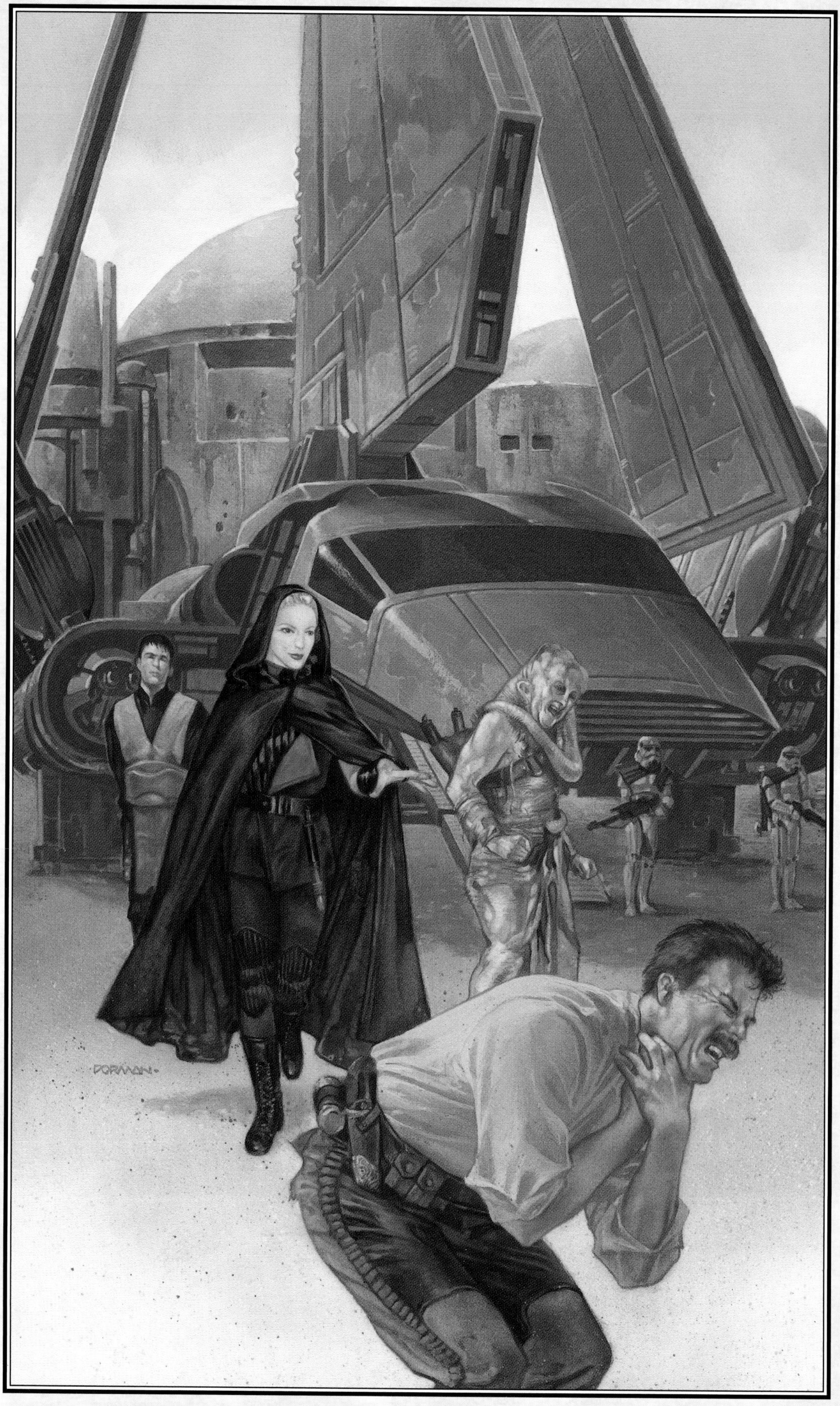
DORMAN

words had gotten him out of trouble before, and they might do so again. "No, no, you've got it all wrong! Give me a chance to explain!"

Sariss looked doubtful. "You *have* an explanation? That seems hard to believe. Still, everyone deserves a chance. That's the Imperial way . . . Take me to your office. You have one, don't you?"

"Oh, yes!" Devo burbled happily. "Follow me . . ."

The crowd parted to let them through. Yun smiled, and Boc laughed.

It took less than an hour for Sariss to pump Devo full of false assurances, drain the politician of relevant information, and confirm her findings through subsequent conversations with Peeno and the tapcafe keeper.

Yun, with assistance from Boc, used the time to survey Fort Nowhere's defenses.

More than 300 pairs of eyes watched the Jedi board their ship and lift off. Mayor Devo, eager to reassert his authority and regain whatever credibility he might have lost, offered an obscene gesture. "That's for you *and* the Emperor!"

The shuttle had just disappeared over the horizon as Peeno sidled up. "So, Byron, what do you think? Why all the interest in ruins and artifacts?"

Devo had small, beady eyes. They darted hither and yon. "Something valuable would be my guess. Something worth sending a task force to Ruusan."

Peeno nodded. "Exactly, so keep it to yourself. Who knows? Maybe *we* can find it."

Devo's eyes glazed over as visions of valuable treasure danced in his head. "It could be ours, Marie! All ours!"

Peeno nodded, wondered if the Imperials were that stupid, and feared that they weren't.

⇒•⇐

The bridge was large and open as befitted a capital ship. Jerec, hands clasped behind his back, stood with his back to the command area. The crew, who occupied semicircular trenches cut into the highly reflective deck, hung on every word. He liked it that way. His voice was pitched to carry. "And your conclusion?"

Sariss, who like Yun and Boc was still aboard the shuttle, brought her report to a close. A holo of her head and shoulders hovered in the air. "So, my lord, based on interviews with members of the criminal community and the squalor in which they are forced to live, it seems safe to conclude that the Valley remains undiscovered."

25

Jerec paused, allowed the tension to build, and nodded his head. "I concur. Destroy the settlement."

⟫◇⟪

The Imperial raiding party had been gathering for more than twenty-six hours. The flat area, surrounded by hills, made a perfect staging area. A maintenance facility had been set up, fuel bladders had been buried, and a perimeter established. It was patrolled by a pair of AT-ST walkers and supported by heavily armed troopers.

The unit, which would depend on speed, surprise, and over-whelming force, consisted of four assault shuttles and six TIE fighters. They were manned by the best the larger task force had to offer and ready for action.

Sariss, her hair whipped by desert wind, took one last look at the ships under her command and spoke into the wire-thin boom mike. "All right, you know the plan. TIE fighters first . . . assault boats second. Let's wind 'em up."

The Jedi felt the ramp bounce under her weight as she entered the ship. She slipped into the co-pilot's position, fastened her harness, and gave the pilot a nod. He ran up the power, pulled back on the controls, and scanned the readouts. The ship rose, rocked in the breeze, and vectored away. The rest of the shuttles followed.

The smugglers had anticipated the possibility of a space-borne attack, which was the reason for the satellites. However, once the orbital surveillance system had been neutralized, and with no ground-based detectors to fall back on, the attack would have caught the colony by surprise if it had not been for the Jedi's visit. Still, even *with* advance warning, they were only partially prepared.

The TIE fighters came first, low and slow, their cannons spitting death. The initial volley punched holes in the rammed earth walls, destroyed the southern gate, and set a storage shed on fire. The smoke made an excellent marker and helped orient the pilots during successive attacks.

The fort's defenses were manned — Peeno had seen to that. Turrets swiveled as gunners tracked the incoming ships, and Dinko whooped with joy. "I nailed one of the slimeballs, lieutenant — look at that!"

Peeno, who was directing the defensive effort from an underground bunker, consulted her monitors. There weren't very many of them, all sitting on an old cargo module, connected by a maze of wires. She watched a TIE fighter explode, saw flaming debris fall on Katarn's Hill, and knew there would be casualties. "Nice shooting, Dinko — keep it up."

"We have four inbound assault shuttles . . . range, thirty klicks."

Peeno didn't recognize the voice — but was thankful for the information. The fort's line-of-sight, target-acquisition system consisted of volunteers equipped with electrobinoculars.

She turned to her weapons-control officer, a grim-faced sixteen-year-old with an aptitude for electronics. "Missile status?"

"Ready . . ."

"Prepare to launch . . . launch."

The youngster tapped some keys. Hatches slid clear, a flight of six missiles soared into the sky and flew down range. "We've got 'em!" the teenager said excitedly. "We've got 'em!"

"Maybe," Peeno replied levelly, "and maybe not. Prepare flight two."

Sariss watched impassively as the first TIE fighter exploded, cursed the pilot for a fool, and felt the shuttle jink to port.

"Blew chaff," the pilot reported laconically. "Surface-to-air missiles inbound . . . air-to-air outbound."

The pilot thumbed a button, and two flights of four missiles raced away. Sariss felt the shuttle jerk and saw reddish-orange flowers populate the sky. The pilot kept count. "Three, four, five . . ."

"And six," Sariss said dryly, as shuttle number three staggered, veered off course, and hit the side of a hill.

Then the fort was below, still fighting, in spite of the fact that three of its ball turrets had been destroyed and that a forty-meter section of wall had been breached.

Antlike figures could be seen running in all directions, while others sought the comparative safety of the underground caves. A TIE fighter swooped in on a strafing run, mowed an entire row of fugitives, and roared away.

"Put her down," Sariss said grimly. "Some of the criminals are getting away."

The pilot nodded, put the ship into a tight turn, and chinned the intercom. "Thirty to dirt . . . stand by."

Forty stormtroopers had been crammed into the cargo area. They pulled one last check on their weapons and waited for the moment of impact. It came with a thump, tone, and green light. Daylight appeared, the ramp fell, and an officer began to yell. "Go! Go! Go!" They went. Ground fire stuttered out to greet them, one fell, and the rest charged.

The shuttle rocked under the impact of a shoulder-launched missile but remained undamaged. Sariss, who was unarmed with the exception of her lightsaber, strolled down the ramp. An energy beam whipped by her head, knocked a trooper off his feet, and left her untouched. That's when she saw Devo, waddling out to meet her, his face contorted with fear. "What are you doing? I answered your questions. You promised to leave us alone!"

The Jedi smiled. "Why, Mayor Devo! Nice to see you again. Politicians tell so many lies that I assumed you knew one when you heard it."

Sariss lit the lightsaber. It crackled and popped. The settler, eyes the size of saucers, tried to retreat. Energy sizzled, and his head flew off his shoulders and rolled down the slope.

It took fifteen minutes to subdue the fort and another twenty to clear the underground caves. Some of the colonists had managed to escape, Sariss knew that, but wasn't inclined to follow. The long and none-too-glamorous job of extermination could be left to junior officers and stormtroopers. Her task was done.

The Jedi waited for Boc to finish off a wounded settler, ordered Yun to destroy the subsurface farms, and climbed a nearby hill. A half-buried dwelling crackled as it burned, a woman lay dead a few feet away, and a gra fought to break its tether.

Sariss gained the summit, looked out across the badlands, and wondered what the planet had been like when the forces of light and darkness had clashed out on the plains. When artificial lightning had split the sky, when Jedi had fallen like wheat before a combine, and the stink of ozone filled the air.

The fact that such battles had occurred was incredible enough, but even more amazing was the fact that the ancient ones were still there — hidden in their Valley — waiting for someone to command their power. Jerec? Yes, probably, but with her at his side.

The wind swept in off the plains, caused her cape to snap, and blew smoke toward the east. The first battle had been fought — and the first battle had been won.

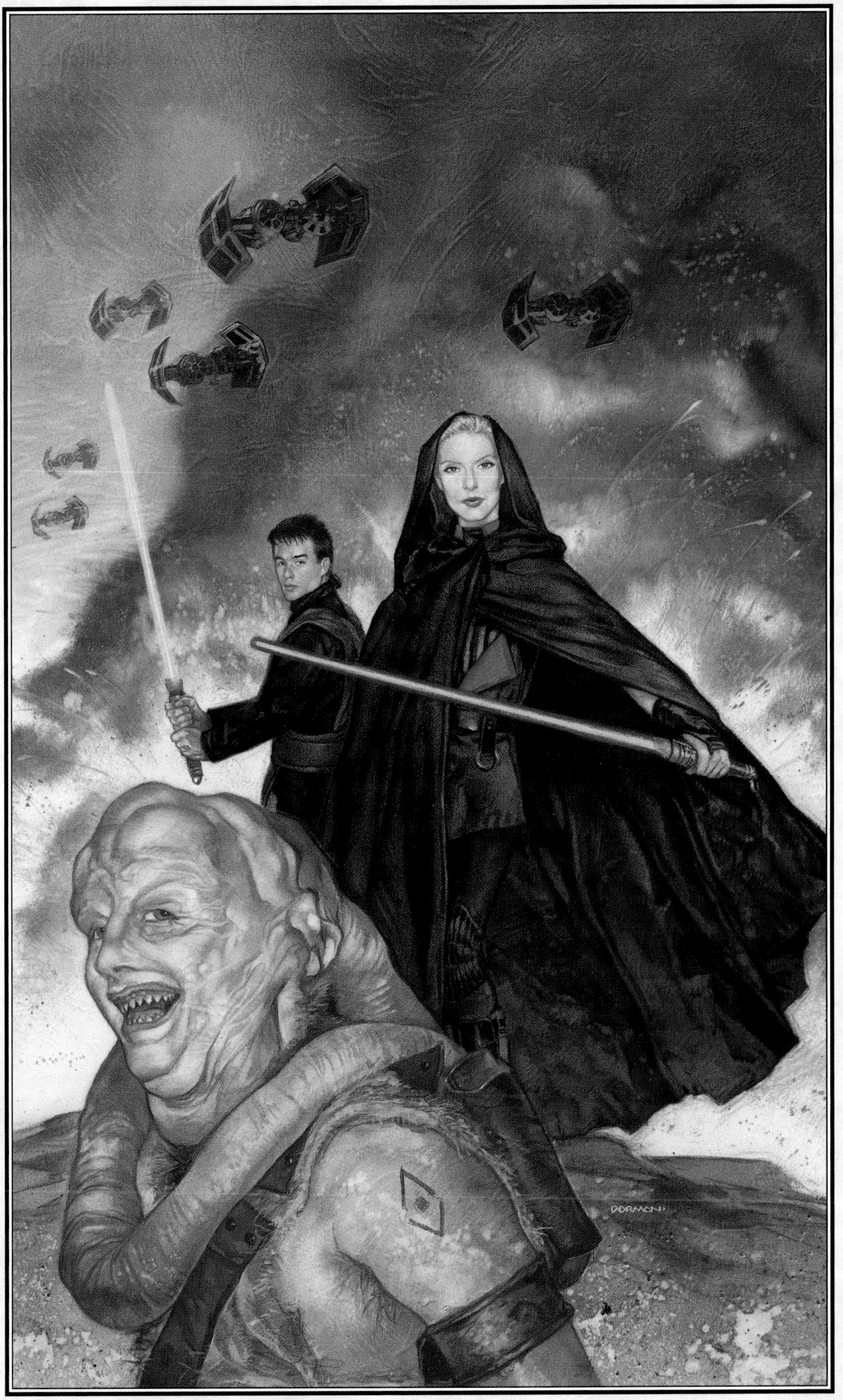
DORMAN

CHAPTER 2

Fire rippled along the *New Hope*'s port side as a squadron of Imperial TIE bombers fought their way through Rebel defenses and launched their proton torpedoes. The deflector shields had gone down ten minutes before — so some of them were bound to get through.

Leia Organa Solo felt the hull shudder, met Mon Mothma's gaze, and knew what she was thinking. The Dreadnaught's best days were behind it. Last stationed over Churba, where it had served as a war museum, the ship had been a symbol of Imperial dominance. A symbol that Rebel forces had stolen and towed away. The victory was largely psychological, but a hull is a hull, and the Rebels needed hulls. That being the case, the Dreadnaught underwent a complete overhaul, was rechristened the *New Hope*, and hurriedly pressed into service.

Still, that being said, the *Hope* was no match for newer vessels half her size and served as a mobile HQ. She'd been in orbit around Milagro for a couple of months now, where she had provided the Rebel command structure with a space-going platform.

That's why both women knew the Dreadnaught wouldn't stand a chance against a Star Destroyer, wondered why the Imperial ship hadn't closed with them, and were thankful it hadn't. TIE bombers were one thing, but the massive weapons the Destroyer could bring to bear were something else. Not that they were about to say anything in front of the bridge crew. Morale was high, and they wanted to keep it that way.

Damage reports continued to flood in. "Turbolaser battery fourteen took a direct hit . . ."

"We have a pressure leak in compartment A-Forty-three . . ."

"The port sensor array is gone . . . along with escape pods sixty through sixty-nine . . ."

The bridge crew, under the somewhat stoic command of a Mon Calamari named Captain Tola, acknowledged the reports and assigned appropriate resources to deal with them.

Mon Mothma, her hair still damp from a hastily interrupted shower, looked composed as usual. A silver pin secured her robe, which hung in orderly folds. "Any news from General Solo?"

Leia knew the question was rhetorical but answered anyway. "No, all three squadrons should be on the far side of Milagro by now, preparing to slingshot around."

Mon Mothma nodded absently. There was so much to consider. The first of the three squadrons belonged to the *Hope* and consisted of crack pilots in nearly new X-wing starfighters. Squadrons two and three were something else again. The pilots, many of whom were still recovering from wounds received earlier, had been recruited off the hospital ship *Mercy* and ferried down to Milagro's surface. Once there they were assigned a mishmash of old Y-wings, reconditioned X-wings, and, miracle of all miracles, two B-wings, just cleared for battle.

It was these forces, under the command of General Han Solo, that would decide the battle. *If* they could find the Star Destroyer from which the TIE bombers had been launched, and *if* they could neutralize it. Adding to the urgent need for a Rebel victory was the fact that a Battle Group had been dispatched six days before. A force that could return victorious or badly mauled and in need of support.

All of which raised another question: Had the Imperials known the *New Hope* was vulnerable? And if so, how? Had a probe droid stumbled across their hiding place? Had the Imperials planted a spy in the Rebel command structure? Mon Mothma sighed. The possibilities were endless . . . and explained why she rarely got enough sleep.

A familiar voice came over one of the ship-to-ship comm channels. "Solo here . . . we're approaching the North Pole and about to break the planetary horizon. Give us the latest."

A powerful computer had been used to analyze Imperial attack vectors, comm traffic, and exit paths. And it was that information, combined with stats on the TIE bombers' power plants and fuel consumption, that would provide the Rebel attack force with the Star Destroyer's probable location. Or so they hoped, since the best way to prevent the capital ship from launching TIEs or engaging the *New Hope* directly, was to take her out or, failing that, to chase her away.

The Rebel starfighters broke the planetary horizon, received the information they needed, and altered course. "Got it," the voice confirmed. "Keep my dinner warm. Over."

Leia smiled, knew the comment was directed to her, and remembered the meal she and Han had nearly shared. There had been wine, candles, and the possibility of . . .

A hand touched Leia's arm. She turned, reached out to steady the comm tech as the Dreadnaught took another hit, and smiled reassuringly. "Yes?"

"A comm call for you, ma'am," the young man stuttered, "from your brother."

Leia frowned. "From Luke? Are you sure?"

"Yes, ma'am," the tech nodded emphatically. "He's on frequency six — channel four."

Luke Skywalker had left the Dreadnaught two weeks earlier, first to carry out a mission of his own, then to check on Kyle Katarn and Jan Ors.

After obtaining plans that enabled the Alliance to destroy the Imperial Death Star, the agents had taken on a new mission: the search for the Valley of the Jedi. A mission Skywalker considered important and hoped would succeed. Now he had returned — and at the worst possible time.

Leia hurried to a console and the holo of Luke Skywalker's face. He wore a helmet and flight suit. "Luke! Turn back! We're under attack!"

"No kidding," the Jedi said dryly. "We noticed. A pair of TIE fighters jumped us as we left hyperspace. We nailed 'em, but it looks like there are more up ahead."

" 'We'?"

"The *Moldy Crow* is off my starboard wing. Kyle Katarn and Jan Ors send their best."

"Break it off," Leia urged. "There are too many of them between you and us. Han and three squadrons of starfighters are looking for the Imperial Destroyer now."

"Too late," Skywalker said laconically. "We found it . . . or they found us! She's a Destroyer all right, Imperial class by the look of her, with bow damage. I see plenty of escorts . . . thirty, maybe more. Could be worse, though, since at least half appear to be transports."

"What was that?" Mon Mothma demanded, appearing at Leia's side. "Did Luke say 'damaged'?"

"I sure did," Skywalker answered. "I see major damage to the Destroyer's bow — as if something hit her or she hit it. Han can home on my transponder while we give her something to think about."

Mon Mothma brought her fist down on the console. A stylus jumped in response. "That's it! That's why the Destroyer didn't come after us — she's damaged! She dropped into this system looking for a place to hide and found us waiting for her! Captain Tola! Inform General Solo and prepare to break orbit."

If Tola was upset by the manner in which a civilian ordered him around, he gave no sign of it. Orders were given, the Dreadnaught broke orbit, and the counterattack began.

The *Hope* lurched as an Imperial pilot lost control of his fighter and slammed into the hull. The explosion destroyed cooling stack three and burned itself out. The lights flickered, steadied, and held. Mon Mothma looked at Leia. "It's going to be close."

The younger woman nodded, felt her fingernails bite into the palms of her hands, and fought to maintain her composure. "Yes, very close indeed."

<hr>

The *Moldy Crow* did a wing over as Jan Ors fought to stay on Luke Skywalker's tail. The Jedi Knight's X-wing was smaller, faster, and a good deal more maneuverable than the Corellian-built ship.

Originally designed to carry small but critical cargoes to asteroid miners and orbital space stations, the *Crow* had served many purposes since then, many of which weren't exactly legal. That being the case, she could deliver a fair turn of speed and carried more armament than most ships her size. Something for which Jan was thankful — given Luke Skywalker's seemingly suicidal decision to engage what looked like half the Imperial Navy.

"Here they come!"

The transmission seemed somewhat unnecessary, given the number of targets that filled her view screen. Jan resisted the temptation to duck as coherent energy blipped over the *Crow's* hull and began the endless journey into space.

Skywalker fired in return and had the satisfaction of seeing one enemy ship explode and another tumble out of control as Jan added the weight of her weapons to his.

Kyle Katarn sat in the co-pilot's seat, wished he had something to do, and ground his teeth in frustration. The *Crow* was *his* ship, but Jan had been at the controls when the fight started, and there was no acceptable way to usurp her position. Not that such a move would made much sense since she was the better pilot.

All of which left Kyle helpless . . . or did it? Unlike most Jedi, who serve an apprenticeship under a Master, Kyle had been forced to work on his talents on his own, or *almost* on his own, since he did receive occasional guidance from the now-disembodied Jedi known as Rahn.

And among the many things Kyle had learned was the fact that there is no weapon more powerful than an open mind.

Take the present situation for example: There was an opportunity somewhere in front of him, and all he had to do was find it. The situation reminded Kyle of the set-piece battles he'd been required to study at the Imperial Military Academy. A career he had pursued in order to get an education — but abandoned after his father had been murdered. Murdered and his head placed on a spike for all to see. Kyle hadn't been there, but he'd seen a holo, and the image haunted his dreams.

The Imperial Star Destroyer seemed to swell in size. Support ships surrounded the larger vessel and opened fire. Kyle saw that they had formed a protective globe around the Destroyer, which, though heavily armed, was temporarily vulnerable due to the bow damage and the ongoing need to launch and retrieve TIE fighters — many of which were occupied elsewhere.

Suddenly Kyle had it, the perfect place to hide, even though the enemy would know exactly where they were. Not forever — just long enough for the Rebel fighters to arrive.

"Jan! Luke! Go for the center of their formation. Get between the Destroyer and her escorts, and maintain that position as long as you can."

Skywalker put the X-wing into a tight turn, fired at a TIE fighter, noticed it was one of the newer models — a GT if memory served him correctly — and considered the agent's suggestion. The idea seemed suicidal at first — until the beauty of it struck him. By placing themselves between the capital ship and her escorts, they would force the Imperials to break formation, fire at each other in an attempt to hit the Rebel ships, or cease firing altogether! "Good idea, Kyle . . . *if* we can get there in one whole piece. I'm going in . . ."

Han Solo checked to make sure that the Rebel attack group was still closing on course, saw that they were, and turned to his companion. "Let's run a last-minute check, Chewie — how's that power coupler? I'd sure hate to have it burn out with a couple of TIE fighters on our tails."

Though able to understand Basic, Chewbacca wasn't equipped to speak it. He growled resentfully, stabbed at some buttons, and pointed at a display.

Han frowned. "Yeah, I can read, but just because it looks good *now* doesn't mean it'll stay that way."

Chewbacca made a moaning sound, started to release his harness, and stopped when a voice came over the group's comm frequency. "Medpac One to Group Leader . . ."

Han smiled. There had been very little time for niceties such as call signs. That being the case, the second squadron, mainly comprised of walking wounded, had chosen their own. "I read you, Medpac One . . . go. Over."

"The bandits are coming out to play . . . twenty . . . maybe more. Over."

Han cursed the need for the *Millennium Falcon* to lag behind, protected by a screen of Y-wings, and wished he could see the enemy for himself. It didn't make sense though — not with such a makeshift unit. Leadership would be crucial, and there wouldn't be any if he were killed during the first few minutes of battle. "Roger that . . . you'll see even more as they pull fighters off the *Hope* and send 'em our way. Remember, don't let the Imps suck us into multiple dog fights. Go for the Destroyer."

"Roger," Medpac One said with a cheerfulness he really didn't feel. "Engaging now."

The next fifteen minutes were some of the longest in Han's life. Medpac One and his squadron absorbed the initial attack, lost two X-wings, and bored through. The weight of three full squadrons, no matter how iffy some of the individual ships might be, was hard to resist.

The officer in charge of the Imperial Task Force continually sent two-ship flights in to pull Rebel fighters away and thereby weaken the counterattack.

Han, who had the instincts of a loner and had never enjoyed following other people's orders, found himself in the somewhat ironic position of maintaining ironclad discipline. Pilots who succumbed to temptation, or were cut off through no fault of their own, were left to fend for themselves as the larger force broke through wave after wave of TIE fighters. Minidramas, too many to count, played themselves out.

"Break right, Medpac Three! There's one on your tail."

"Yahoo! Eat energy, you scum-sucking Imperial . . ."

"Watch your six . . . two on the way."

"Hey, you! In the Y-wing . . . follow me."

"It hurts . . . it hurts so bad . . ."

"I'm on it, Blue Six . . . keep her steady . . ."

Then, through the mishmash of comm traffic, Han heard what he'd been waiting for. "Medpac Four to Group Leader . . . I have a visual on the Imperial Task Force . . . repeat . . . a visual on the Imperial Task Force."

Han sideslipped to avoid the remains of a TIE fighter, fired at another, and sent a thought toward Luke. "Hang in there, kid . . . we're almost there . . ."

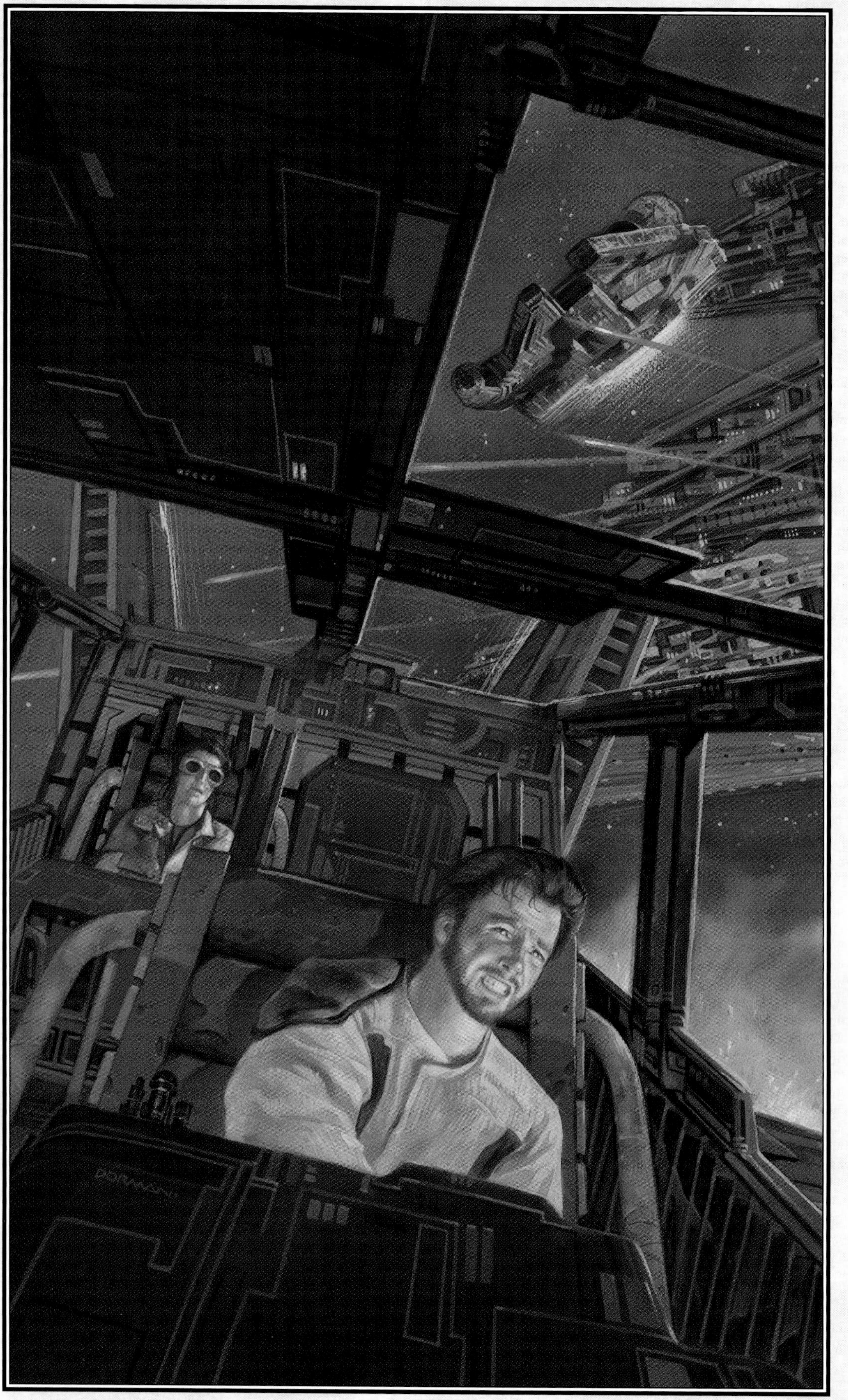
DORMAN

The X-wing rocked from side to side, dodged laser fire, and bored in. Luke could almost hear Yoda's voice: "Have a pattern things do, starting with the subatomic structure of the pebble in your hand and extending to the stars themselves. Hmmm, yes. Find the pattern, understand the manner in which it was woven, and nothing shall stand in your way."

Each of the Imperial ships had its own fire-control center, and all of those centers had been slaved to a computer aboard the Destroyer. While this strategy made maximum use of the Task Force's weaponry, it also created a pattern that Luke could *feel*.

The trick was to direct his mind toward understanding the individual subpatterns that contributed to the whole but to do so without conscious thought, because conscious thought took time and led to doubt. That being the case, Luke "sensed" where to direct his ship, fired when instinct told him to do so, and wove his way through a maze of outgoing laser fire. The *Moldy Crow*, still in one piece and still on Luke's tail, followed behind.

Jan, her hands dancing between controls, spoke from the side of her mouth. "Did you see that? It's as if he *knows* which way to go."

Kyle, who had made a good deal of progress where his own talents were concerned, nodded admiringly. "That's because he *does* know which way to go. Stay on his tail."

Jan triggered the ship's cannons, winced as the *Crow* sped through the resulting explosion, and watched the Destroyer grow in size. The Rebel ships had penetrated the outer screen by then and were passing through the second.

Lights flashed as a chunk of TIE fighter hit the deflector shield, caused an overload, and spun away.

———— ❧ ————

Imperial Naval Captain Purdy M. Trico watched the holo screens, listened to the comm traffic, and wondered why the gods had decided to abandon him. A hand strayed to a bulge in his uniform. The amulet had always worked before — what had changed?

The Imperial power structure frowned on gods, *any* sort of gods, especially those believed to have more power than the state. But that hadn't stopped Trico from worshiping the same entities his forefathers had, not at the Academy, where such worship could result in expulsion, and not during the subsequent years when discovery would have ruined his career.

So why had the gods deserted him during his hour of need? Why had Mugg, Bron, and the great Pula allowed the Rebel gunship to ram his Destroyer? And then, when he sought the relative safety of a war-ravaged solar system, why had they cursed him with a Dreadnaught? Not to mention the swarm of hostile fighters? Even now, two Rebel ships were drilling in through his defenses as if protected from all harm. The reverie, which had lasted little more than a few seconds, ended as the sometimes-meddlesome executive officer vied for his attention. "Sorry to bother you, sir . . . but the Rebel Dreadnaught broke orbit and is headed this way."

Trico came from a heavy gravity world and, being of the fourth generation, had the physique of a meter-and-a-half-tall weight lifter. Muscles bunched and writhed as he fought the impulse to twist the other officer's head off. " 'Has' broken orbit? Did you say 'has'? Why wasn't I notified when this evolution began?"

The XO found it difficult to swallow. Though more competent than some, Trico had a reputation as something of a martinet, and a volatile one at that. "Because our fighters were trying to intercept the Rebels . . . sir."

Trico could hear the gods laughing. He forced his voice to remain steady. "You allowed that? None of our fighters were detailed to monitor the Dreadnaught? A vessel that, though dated, has plating thicker than ours and mounts major offensive weapons?"

The XO started to tremble. "It wasn't my fault . . . I thought . . ."

A hole appeared at the center of the executive officer's forehead, and his eyes crossed as he was trying to get a look at it. The body made a thumping sound as it hit the deck.

Trico holstered his weapon and looked up to find that the Rebel ships, the two he had observed earlier, had not only penetrated his innermost defenses, they'd done so with impunity. His index finger trembled as he pointed at the holo. "What are you waiting for? Destroy them!"

"Yes, sir," the weapons-control officer replied shakily. "Shall we destroy our escorts as well?" The question *sounded* insubordinate — but wasn't.

Trico looked again, realized that the Rebs had taken their positions on purpose, and swore a terrible oath. "Pula, take them! I'll teach the dogs some respect . . . break formation!"

The entire bridge crew knew it was a mistake, but no one had the courage to say so. Not with the XO's body still where it had fallen. Orders were given, relayed to the proper parties, and acted upon. Slowly, with a dignity befitting a ship of her size and importance, a gap opened between the Destroyer and her escorts.

Luke saw the movement, knew what it meant, and opened his throttles. The X-wing shot forward. "Jan! Kyle! Follow me!"

Jan shoved the throttles to their stops, felt the gee forces push her back into the seat, and uttered a silent prayer.

Energy pulsed outward as the Destroyer fired her main batteries and the escorts did likewise. The glare created by the ravening beams of energy caused the view screens to darken and left the Rebels blind. Their deflector shields flared to the edge of burnout and held. Time seemed to slow . . .

———»-◦-«———

"Group Leader to Command," Han said evenly. "We have closed with the enemy and are about to engage. The Destroyer broke formation. Her deflector shields are down in order to retrieve fighters, and she's firing away from us. I recommend that you bring the *Hope* into action."

Mon Mothma looked at Captain Tola and waited for the Mon Calamari's judgment. It had been an error to order the ship out of orbit without consulting him. . . . and one which she refused to repeat. Yes, she knew what *she* would do, but the decision was his.

Leia held her breath, was thankful that the decision belonged to someone else, and did her best to appear unconcerned.

Captain Tola, well aware of the silence that had descended over the bridge, gave a nod. The Dreadnaught might be a museum piece, but the odds were as good as they were likely to get. "You heard the general — this is the chance we've been waiting for! There's a Destroyer out there — let's give her a history lesson."

———»-◦-«———

Captain Trico was furious. "You missed them, blast your worthless hide! Two ships and you missed them both! You are incompetent, sir, and a disgrace to this ship."

"The Dreadnaught means to engage, sir," the weapons-control officer replied desperately. "I recommend we rejoin our escorts — or take the entire Task Force into hyperspace."

"And leave more than a hundred TIE pilots to die?" Captain Trico demanded coldly. "Have you lost your mind? Or just your nerve?"

Trico was reaching for his sidearm, preparing to eliminate still another incompetent, when a comm tech interrupted. "Here they come, sir! Rebel fighters followed by the Dreadnaught!"

Trico spun, his face contorted in anger, his right index finger pointed like a gun. The entire bridge crew blanched. "You will stand and fight! I will shoot the first man to leave his post!"

The weapons-control officer watched his subordinates from the corners of his eyes, knew they wouldn't back him, and turned to the control consoles. "You heard the captain. Let's get to work."

The ensuing battle lasted more than three hours . . . but was never really in doubt. Cut off from her escorts, and with only a handful of TIE fighters to defend her, the Destroyer was not only weakened but downright vulnerable. Still, the Imperials continued to fight, not valiantly, but because Trico insisted that they do so.

Finally, after the hull had been repeatedly breached and more than half the laser batteries silenced, the weapons officer, knowing that the bridge recorders had captured his commanding officer's eccentric behavior and confident that the crew were now ready to support him, took matters into his own hands.

Captain Trico was in midrant, screaming the names of his gods, when the blaster bolt bored through his brain. An offer of unconditional surrender followed two minutes later.

—⇒∘⇐—

The turbolift came to a halt, doors rolled open, and the Rebels stepped out into the corridor. Kyle took two steps and stopped. Jan bumped into him. She was about to say something when she saw why.

More than a hundred Imperial fighters had attacked the *Hope* . . . but this was the only one that had penetrated the bulkhead. The ship's solar panels had been ripped off, but the nose jutted into the passageway. The pilot, still visible within, sat slumped at his controls. His visor had been raised, and Jan saw he was little more than a boy, just one of the hundreds who had died during the twelve-hour battle. The voice came from beside her. It belonged to a rating in a smoke-stained uniform. He held a fusion cutter in his hand and was part of a damage-control party.

"Weird, huh? We took a torp in that same spot, it blew a hole through the hull, and the fighter plugged it five minutes later. All we had to do was fill the gaps with emergency sealer — pressurize the passageway — and presto! A perfect patch! Something to tell the kids about."

Jan nodded politely, thought about the grandchildren the Imperial pilot would never have, and followed Kyle down the corridor. She had killed men like the pilot, a lot of them, and wished it would end.

Kyle was forced to duck under temporary cable runs, squeeze around repair crews, and give way to high-priority repair droids. The air stank of ozone, sealer, and smoke. In spite of the fact that the Dreadnaught had taken a beating, the agent was struck by the friendly grins, nods, and waves from those he passed. They had taken losses, painful losses, but emerged victorious. The story would grow in the telling — and live long after they were gone.

The sentries stationed in front of Mon Mothma's day cabin checked

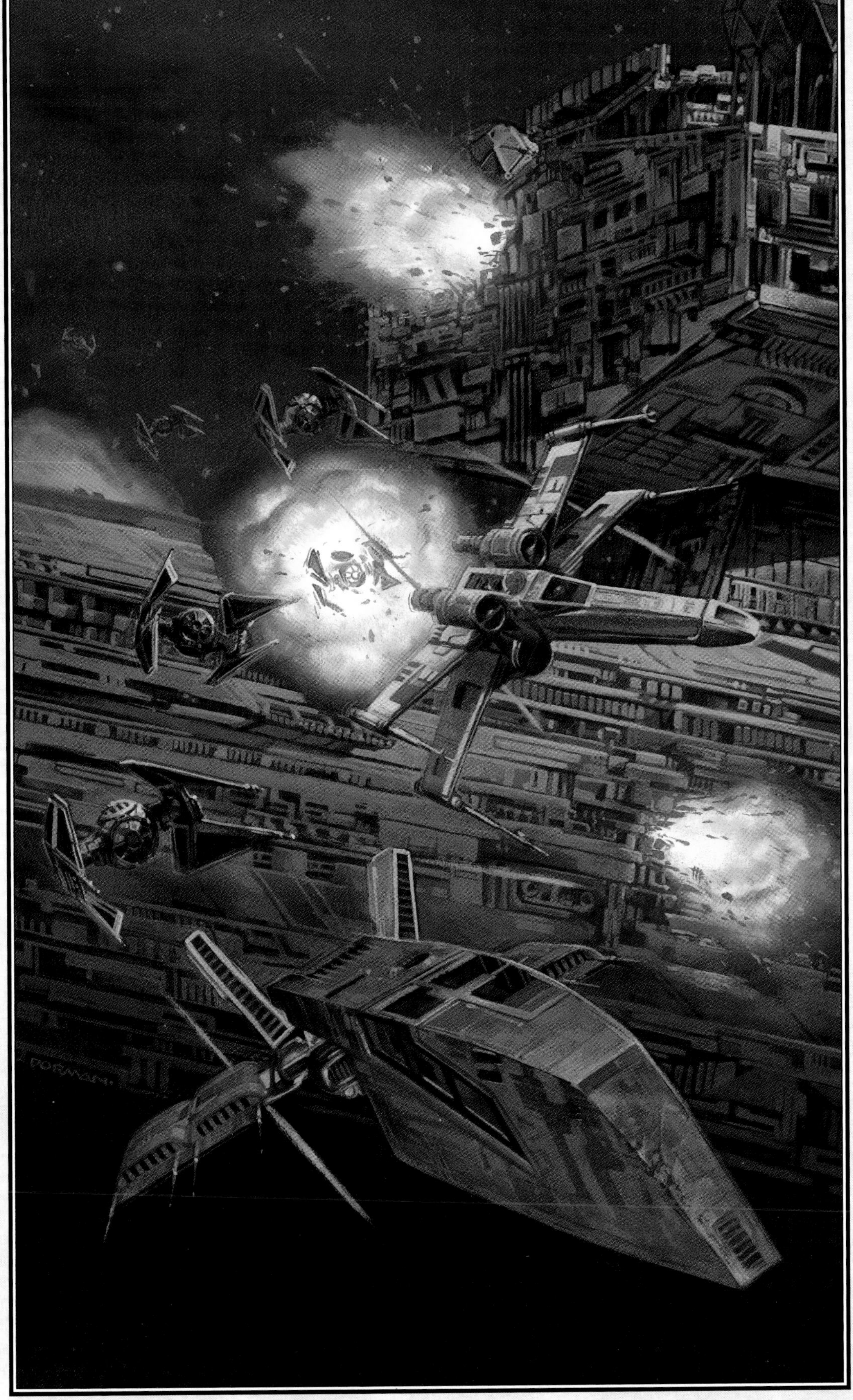

credentials and, much to Kyle's surprise, permitted him to retain both his sidearm and lightsaber. An indication of trust that he, unlike those who accompanied him, had never been accorded before.

Jan knew what he was thinking and winked. Kyle grinned in response. Jan, more than anyone he had ever known, could read his mind. Their hands touched, and Luke, who was last to pass through the door, couldn't help but smile. These two had been made for each other . . . and he hoped they would live long enough to pursue the possibilities.

The compartment had been designed to accommodate the needs of admirals with largely ceremonial duties. That being the case, it was huge. In spite of the fact that the ship had been through a complete overhaul the year before, there were scant resources to squander on decor. The hangings, many of which were hundreds of years old, seemed badly out of place. Especially given the current occupant's unostentatious style. Mon Mothma, whom Kyle had met before, came forward to greet him. "Kyle . . . it's good to see you again. Jan . . . how are you? You know Leia . . . Have you met Han Solo?"

Jan hadn't, although she had certainly heard of him, and shook hands.

Luke hugged Leia and turned toward Kyle. "Kyle, I would like to introduce my sister, Leia Organa Solo, and Han Solo."

Kyle shook hands and tried to ignore the fact that they were famous. Both looked the way he felt: tired and more than a little haggard. Mon Mothma called the meeting to order. "I know everyone could use some sleep, so let's get on with it. Han, I assume Leia briefed you on this, but don't hesitate to ask questions.

"Kyle, Luke tells me that you not only confirmed that the Valley of the Jedi exists, you managed to obtain the coordinates for it. Congratulations! The Alliance owes you yet another debt of gratitude."

Kyle remembered the nearly fatal trip down into the depths of Nar Shaddaa, the looting of his father's farm, the duel with the Dark Jedi Yun, the confrontation with the droid 8t88, the battle with Gorc and Pic, and the rather unpleasant place from which the coordinates had eventually been retrieved. The fact that Mon Mothma could summarize the whole thing in a single sentence amazed him. Still, from her point of view, it was results that counted. He shrugged. "Thanks, but Jan deserves at least half the credit."

Blood colored Jan's cheeks, and Mon Mothma smiled. "As a matter of fact it was Jan, with a significant amount of help from Leia and Luke, who convinced me to turn you loose on the problem, or didn't you know that?"

Kyle *wasn't* aware of that, although he might have guessed, since Mon Mothma had traditionally been suspicious of his motives. It was his turn to blush, and it was Han who responded. "Don't let it bother you, kid . . . they don't trust *me* either!"

Everyone laughed including Mon Mothma. "So, Kyle, we know where the Valley is located. Now what?"

Kyle had anticipated the moment and prepared his speech. "A battle was fought on the planet Ruusan more than a thousand years ago. A battle fought between two armies of Jedi. Somehow," and here the agent looked at Luke, "and no one is sure how, the power represented by these armies became trapped within a Valley.

"A Dark Jedi named Jerec stole the coordinates from my father's farm and has no doubt made use of them. *If* he can tap the power invested there, *if* he can control it, we will witness the birth of an Empire that will make this one seem enlightened by comparison."

"Yes," Mon Mothma said impatiently, "we're aware of the threat. What do you think we should *do* about it?"

Kyle wasn't so sure that Han knew all the facts . . . but decided to let the comment pass. "I propose to go there, with Jan if she's willing, and find a way to stop him. We did it on Danuta . . . and we can do it again."

Mon Mothma considered the mission to Danuta. It had been a long shot, but the agents had located the Death Star plans and brought them out. An accomplishment that, when combined with information secured by others, enabled the Rebels to win the Battle of Yavin. The twosome had been lucky, *very* lucky, and the odds were against them being that lucky again.

"I admire your bravery, Kyle, not to mention your dedication to the Rebel cause, but the odds are stacked against you. You can bet that Jerec has a Destroyer, who knows how many support vessels, and plenty of troops. No, what we need is a fully equipped Battle Group."

"A nice thought," Leia said gently, "but where would it come from? We're stretched thin as it is."

"True," Mon Mothma acknowledged thoughtfully, "but consider the alternative. How would Kyle and Jan make their way past the picket ships? And even if they did, what would they do on the surface? Very little is known about the planet, but one thing is for sure: There's no civilian population in which to hide."

Luke had a distant almost dreamy expression. It was he who broke the ensuing silence. "Everything Mon Mothma says is true . . . but truth has many levels. The power that Jerec seeks to control flows from spirits trapped within the Valley . . . spirits who *must* be freed. If Kyle freed the spirits, the threat would disappear. All without the use of a Battle Group. Easy? No, but there is a flow to such things, a flow with power of its own." The Jedi eyed those around him.

"I am told there is a species of sentients on Ruusan, a species with a long history, much of which has been captured in something they refer to as the poem of ages. There are numerous prophecies toward the end of the poem, including one that reads, 'And a knight shall come, a battle will be fought, and the prisoners go free.' They believe that it refers to the Valley — and I agree."

Kyle had heard those words before, but he still felt a chill run down his spine and wondered if he should feel proud or very, very frightened. The second possibility seemed more logical.

Mon Mothma sighed. Yes, she knew that there was more to life than what she could hear, touch, taste, feel, and see. She knew that certain individuals, Luke being an excellent example, had what might be described as additional senses. But *knowing* it, and being comfortable with it, were two different things. She preferred *direct* access to relevant data where important decisions were concerned — and this decision was extremely important. Still, if Luke said something was so, it generally was. She forced a smile. "Okay, given the problems mentioned earlier, how would Kyle and Jan reach the planet's surface?"

Han cleared his throat. His voice was hoarse after more than twelve hours of giving orders. "While it's true that the picket ships would stop one of *our* vessels, an Imperial ship would make it through."

Kyle was quick to seize on the idea. "Han is right! We could stow the *Crow* on one of the captured transports, deliver some supplies, and slip away . . . It's perfect!"

"Not so fast," Mon Mothma said cautiously. "Give the Imperials *some* credit. The transport would be challenged and, lacking the proper recognition codes, searched."

"True," Jan put in, "but every commanding officer wants all the supplies he or she can lay their hands on, especially where munitions are concerned. If a transport drops out of hyperspace and offers them a load of proton torpedoes, the Imperials will jump on it. Especially if the ship and crew seem legit."

Mon Mothma raised an eyebrow. "'Proton torpedoes'? You've got to be kidding . . . How 'bout field rations instead?"

"Some field rations are just as lethal," Han said jokingly, "but I understand your concern. How 'bout some *special* torpedoes? The kind that explode in the launch tube?"

"Exactly what I had in mind," Jan agreed. "Is it settled then?"

Mon Mothma looked around the table and saw each head nod in turn. She added her approval to all the rest. "One last question. Who's going to crew the transport? And even more importantly, who will command it?"

"I volunteer to command," Han responded quickly. "This could be fun."

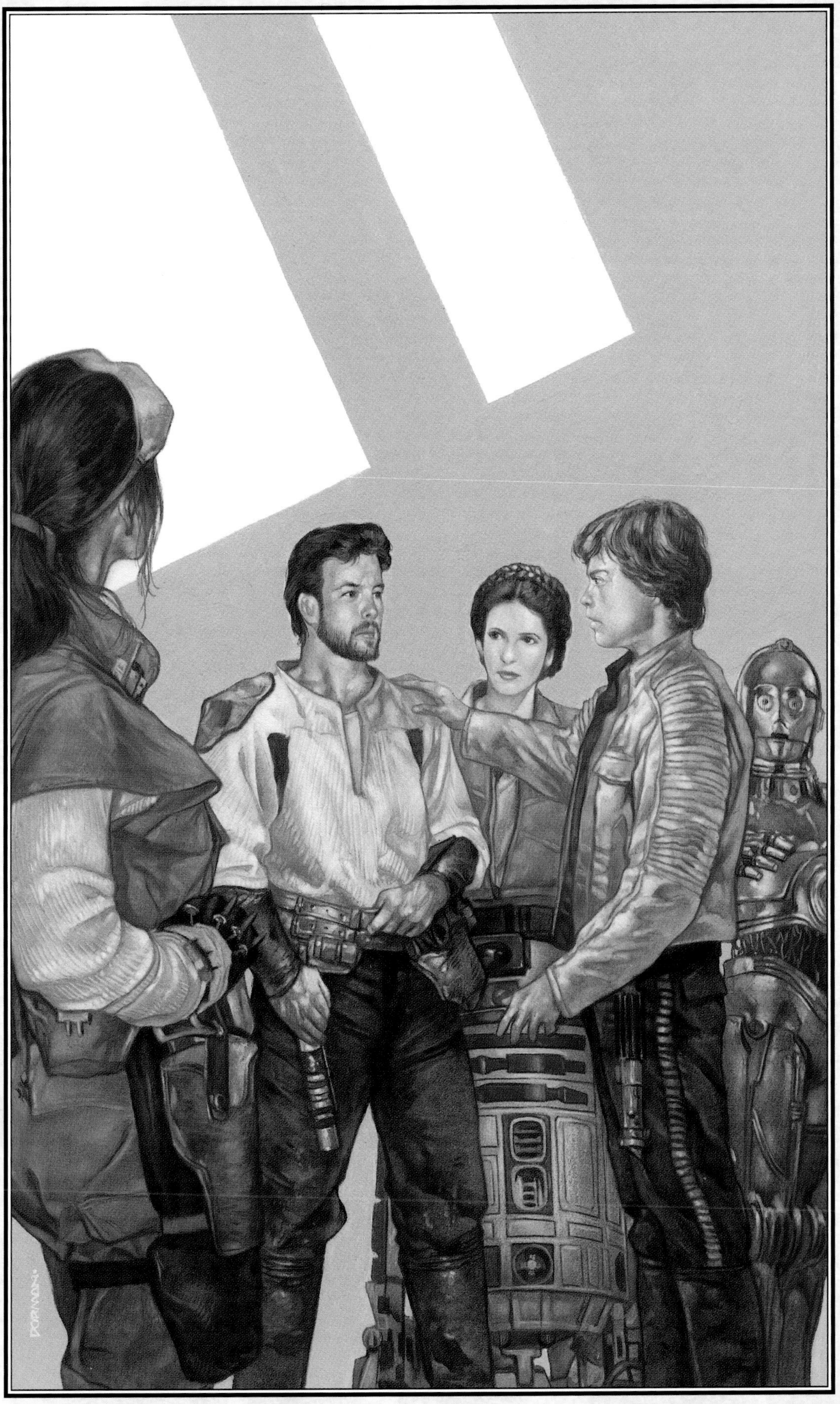
DORMAN

"*And* time consuming," Mon Mothma added cautiously. "We can't afford to let you go right now."

Leia, conscious that she was more than a little biased, nodded in agreement. Han looked in her direction but chose to remain silent.

"I'll find some volunteers," Jan put in. "Folks with Special Ops experience."

"Fine," Mon Mothma said, glad to delegate at least one task to someone else. "Final comments?"

"Just one," Kyle responded soberly. "Wish us luck . . . I have a feeling we're gonna need it."

CHAPTER 3

Sunlight rippled across a sea of shimmering glass. Glass that had once been part of iridescent domes, towering minarets, soaring archways, vertical towers, and all the other structures that constitute a city. A city reduced to a sea of manmade lava, as Imperial laser cannon carved swathes of destruction through the once-beautiful metropolis.

The resulting slag was thicker where buildings had been clustered and thinner out toward the suburbs, where the military base had been established.

The past could still be seen, on a hill where a nearly translucent temple glittered with emerald beauty, on a rise where a half-melted statue stretched a hand toward the heavens, and out on the silicone plain where isolated groups of dwellings remained untouched.

Prisoner 272-20-136 released the T-shaped handlebars and waited for the impact hammer to fall silent. Then, careful of what he was doing, the man took air deep into his lungs and pulled the mask away from his face. Milagro had a thin atmosphere, which was why he and the other prisoners were allowed to work without leg irons. There was nowhere to go — not without air.

The prisoner wiped his forehead with a rag, allowed elastic bands to pull the mask against his face, and checked the seal. The air left a coppery taste in his mouth. The comm set was part of the head gear — and the factory-issued voice was part of his life.

"That was an unauthorized break, Unit 136. Twenty-seven seconds will be deducted from your next rest period."

The prisoner looked back over his shoulder and saw that a detainment droid had approached from behind. It looked like a floating garbage can and had a personality to match. "My name is Obota — Alfonso Obota — Al to my friends."

"No," the droid replied unemotionally, "that's who you *used* to be and may become again. At this particular moment you are Unit 136 — and the most likely member of my crew to be disciplined. Please return to work."

Obota started to object and thought better of it. He had enough trouble without making more. The prisoner took the handlebars and made the hammer dance. The comm mast required six anchors, each sunk into the subsurface strata and fused in place. His task was to drill down through a three-meter-thick mantle of fused glass.

The drill rattled dully, the noise muffled by the thin atmosphere. Glass projectiles peppered the lower part of Obota's legs. They stung, but he knew better than to stop. The hole was a little more than one meter deep when the voice boomed into his ears. "They want you in the admin hut, Unit 136 . . . on the double."

Surprised, but happy to get off work, Obota started to jog. Everything the prisoners did was carried out "on the double." Failure to comply would almost certainly result in punishments that the nearly identical detainment droids dispensed with machine-like consistency.

The base hadn't existed three months before and consisted of sixty-three prefab buildings. It was a sprawling affair that included a landing strip, repair facility, surface-to-air missile batteries, barracks, and a military detention facility.

Normally busy, the place seemed even busier in the aftermath of the battle, as ground personnel struggled to service battle-scarred starfighters, a somber-looking burial party made their way toward a row of recently excavated graves, and an infantry company marched the width of a lavender parade ground.

Building twenty-three served as headquarters for the Military Correction Facility, or MCF. It, like the structures on either side, had an external air lock, inflatable walls, and a protective berm.

Obota waited for the lock to open, shared the chamber with an admin droid, and cycled through. The interior was standard-issue puke green. A long list of things you weren't supposed to do scrolled across a reader-board, and the floor, which some other prisoners had buffed to a high gloss, stretched left and right.

The droid, who had privileges the human didn't, chose the hall to the right. The machine's foot cleats made a squeaking noise and left black skid marks on the otherwise immaculate floor. Obota removed his mask, attached it to his belt, and approached the fiberboard door. The sign read:

MCF 63

HONOR THROUGH DISCIPLINE

Knock before you enter.

Obota knocked three times, shouted "Prisoner 272-20-136 reporting as ordered, sir!" and waited for a reply.

"Enter."

Obota opened the door, stepped through, and crashed to attention. A weary-looking officer nodded, consulted his datapad, and looked up again. "Take a left in the hall . . . fourth door on the right. Move it."

Obota yearned to ask "why" but knew better than to do so. "Sir! Yes, sir!"

Obota did a smart about-face, passed through the door, and marched down the hall. The officer watched the door close, wondered what the cloak-and-dagger types wanted with the poor slob, and returned to his work.

Obota marched down the hall, located the proper office, and discovered it was empty. "Hurry up and wait." A phrase that could have served as the *real* motto for the MCF.

There were chairs, and Obota felt the strong urge to sit in one of them but knew it was against the rules. Rules enforced by holo cams mounted high in each corner of the room. That being the case, the prisoner went to parade rest, chose a spot on the perfectly blank wall, and forced himself to stare at it.

A minute passed, followed by five, followed by ten more. Had they forgotten him? Obota was just about to conclude that they had when he heard voices and felt the fiber foam deck vibrate under his boots. He came to attention as the tech sergeant and two civilians entered the office. Not because they rated the courtesy — but because prisoners honored everyone.

Obota decided to ignore the tech sergeant and focus his attention on the civilians. They were the ones who had summoned him — or so he assumed — and they were the ones to worry about. Why had he been summoned? What did they want? There was no way to tell. Both wore nondescript flight suits and neutral expressions. And what was that hanging at the man's side? A lightsaber? Now *that* was unusual.

The sergeant nodded in Obota's direction. "There he is . . . anything else you need from me?"

The woman shook her head. "No, sergeant, we'll take it from here."

The noncom nodded, left the room, and closed the door behind him. The woman consulted a handheld datapad, looked up, and met Obota's gaze. "My name is Jan Ors — this is Kyle Katarn. You are Alfonso Luiz Obota, service number 272-20-136, originally from the Adega System. You

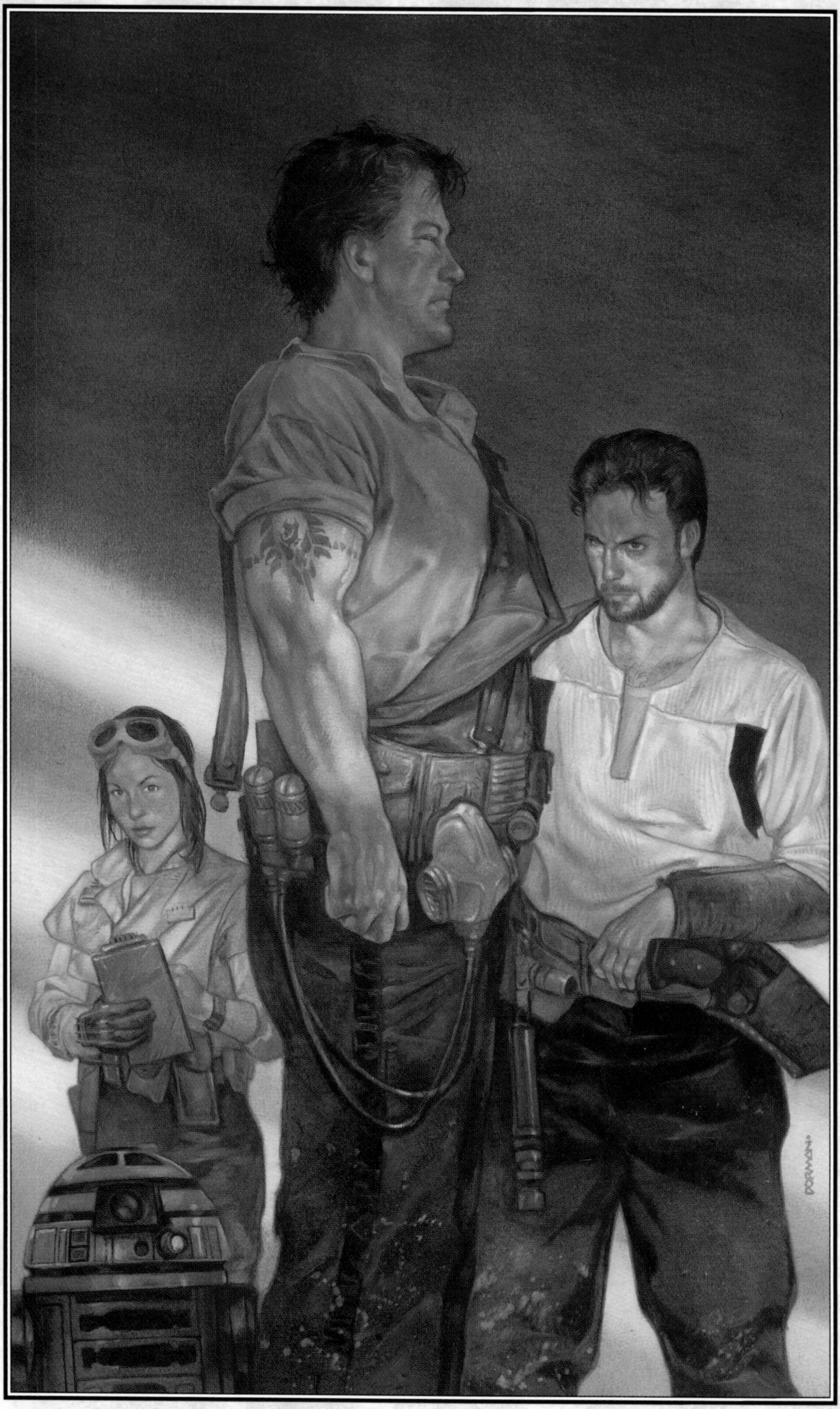
DORMAN

graduated fourth in your class from the Merchant Academy, qualified as third officer on a freighter, and resigned to join the Alliance. That was more than a year ago. You accepted a commission as second lieutenant, became the second officer on a Special Operations transport named the *Pride of Aridus*, and led a mutiny six standard months later. True so far?"

Obota remembered Captain Nord's face, the beads of sweat that dotted his forehead, and the way his hands shook. The *Aridus*, now bearing the name *Spirit of Solaris*, had made ground fall and, under the cover of discharging a completely legitimate cargo, had landed a Special Ops team. They'd been gone for six hours and two minutes, two minutes longer than the insertion plan called for, and Nord wanted to lift. Lift and leave twelve men and women stranded on a planet swarming with Imperial troops. Obota forced his mind to the present. "Ma'am! Yes, ma'am!"

Jan nodded thoughtfully. "The transcript from your court martial says that you refused a legal order, confined your commanding officer to his cabin, and seized control of the ship. True?"

Obota remembered the explosion that momentarily turned night to day. The sound of sirens and the comm call as the Commandos raced for the ship. He remembered Nord screaming at the crew shouting, "Lift! Lift! Lift!" — and his fist connecting with the older officer's chin. It was all a matter of record, captured on the control room recorders and witnessed by the bridge crew. "Ma'am! Yes, ma'am!"

Kyle watched the emotions play across the prisoner's face. He himself was a renegade, a deserter with a price on his head, and could imagine how Obota felt. The conflict between the oath he had sworn and what he knew to be right. Or was it more complicated than that? Captain Nord claimed his second officer had been insubordinate from the start. A self-serving lie? Or a statement of fact?

Jan looked up from her datapad. "The records say that while three of the commandos made it to the *Aridus* and were successfully extracted, TIE fighters attacked your transport above the atmosphere. Five of your fellow crew members were killed during the battle. The ship suffered serious damage and barely made it to hyperspace. Three lives for five . . . a rather poor trade, wouldn't you say?"

Obota remembered the fear, carnage, and smoke. He saw the faces of those who had died, knew they might have lived if he had obeyed orders, and wished he had died in their places. "Ma'am! Yes, ma'am!"

"So," Jan said quietly, "knowing how the whole thing turned out, would you make the same decision again?"

"Ma'am! Yes, ma'am!"

"Why?"

Obota knew the answer — had lain awake countless nights thinking about it — but hesitated. Who were these people? They were covert operations types, that much was obvious, but doing what? And for whom? Knowing would give him an edge, but he *didn't* know and had no way to find out. That being the case, he settled on the truth. "Because it seemed like the right thing to do."

There was silence for a moment. Jan looked at Kyle — and the Jedi considered Obota's words. No complicated excuses, no fancy rationalizations, no self-serving explanations. He smiled. "At ease, Lieutenant Obota, we need an experienced deck officer, and you fit the bill."

The *High Hauler* dropped out of hyperspace and probed the out-of-the-way solar system for ships. There were plenty to find, including a screen of picket ships, a Star Destroyer, numerous escorts, and an alarming number of TIE fighters. Most were centered around the fourth planet from the sun.

Obota, a newly restored lieutenant, but packing the honorary title of "captain," felt something heavy hit the bottom of his stomach. Yes, he'd been expecting to find an Imperial Battle Group and would have been disappointed if he hadn't, but the sight of all those blips on the detector screens still scared the heck out of him.

The challenge was nearly instantaneous. "This is the Imperial Star Destroyer *Vengeance* . . . identify yourself or be fired on."

"Fighters closing fast, sir," a tech interjected. "An escort frigate broke orbit and is coming for a look-see."

Obota checked the Imperial uniform to ensure that the closures were properly snapped, adjusted the bandage that encircled his head, and scanned the bridge. The bridge crew wore grimy uniforms, blood-stained bandages, and carefully applied makeup. They looked exhausted.

Even the untrained eye would see the makeshift hull patch, the dangling cables, and the fire-blackened control console and know what they meant: The *High Hauler* had been in a fight.

A warrant officer, who bore a striking resemblance to Kyle Katarn, intercepted Obota's glance and gave a cheerful thumbs-up. The deck officer winked, turned toward the holo pickup, and touched a button. "The *Vengeance*? This is Lieutenant Hortu Agar — engineering officer for the Imperial Transport *High Hauler*. I assumed command when Captain Drax and the majority of the bridge crew were killed."

The holo swirled, and a *real* captain appeared. He had narrow-set eyes, a beaklike nose, and a slash-shaped mouth. "Listen carefully, lieutenant whoever-you-are . . . I want recognition codes and I want them *now*."

Would the Destroyer actually fire on them? Obota had pooh-poohed the idea earlier — but had started to wonder. The desperation in his voice was real. "I don't know the codes, sir! They're issued on a need-to-know basis, and engineering officers aren't cleared to receive them! We were on a run to Byss when the Rebels jumped us. We fought — but it was no use. The bridge took a direct hit. So, given the fact that we're carrying a full load of proton torpedoes, I thought . . . "

"Did you say 'proton torpedoes'?" the Imperial inquired.

"Why, yes," Obota replied innocently, "two hundred and fifty proton torpedoes to be exact, straight from the factories in the Corporate Sector. That's why . . . "

"Enough," the officer commanded. "A boarding party will inspect your ship, and, assuming that the facts match your story, emergency repairs will be made. You and your crew performed well, lieutenant . . . and the Empire knows how to show its gratitude."

Obota tried to look modest. "Thank you, sir."

"One more thing," the officer added.

"Sir?"

"What sort of condition is your docking bay in?"

"Fully functional, sir."

"Excellent. We can use those torpedoes . . . Have your crew prepare them for transshipment. A shuttle will take them off."

Obota nodded obediently. "Sir! Yes, sir!"

The Imperial said, "That will be all," and the holo snapped to black.

Obota touched a button, checked to ensure that the comm was truly off, and turned to applause. "A sterling performance," Kyle said admiringly.

"Couldn't have been better," Jan said as she emerged from the shadows. "You missed a career on the stage."

"Thank you," Obota said, bowing from the waist. "But that was little more than the first act. The second act is about to begin, and the audience is on its way."

———※○※———

More than an hour passed between the time the *High Hauler* left hyperspace and the assault shuttle entered the transport's launch bay.

The crew, who had already been through more than twenty simulated boardings off Milagro, were in their places. They had counterfeit IDs, family holo stats, ticket stubs, miscellaneous receipts, and all the other junk people keep in their wallets.

All were human because nonhumans were a rarity on Imperial

military vessels, and, with the exception of Jan Ors, all were male, since very few women had been allowed to serve in the Empire's armed forces.

A ship's complement that was supposed to number twenty-five had been reduced to twelve, a number intended to reflect heavy casualties as well as the fact that it had been a long time since the Empire's navy had enjoyed the luxury of full crews.

Yes, Obota thought to himself, details are important. Did we think of everything? The next hour will tell . . .

Hatches closed and the bay was pressurized as the assault shuttle settled onto the repulsor-blackened deck. Obota waited for the green light, heard the klaxon sound, and opened the lock. Air hissed as pressures equalized. The Rebel slipped through the opening, spotted the officer in charge, and hurried to greet him. "Lieutenant! Are we ever glad to see you! Welcome aboard."

The lieutenant, who saw the entire thing as something of a lark, smiled and shook hands. "Looks like you've been through a lot . . . sorry about the formalities."

Jan watched the interchange from the *Crow*'s darkened cockpit and fiddled with a jury-rigged comm set. Obota and the lieutenant were getting along just fine . . . but how 'bout the rest of the boarding party? Their faces were hidden behind armor and visors. The only way to know what they were saying was to monitor their conversations . . . and that's where the comm set came in.

The inspection was cursory at best — and lasted about forty-five minutes. After a quick tour of the bridge, a stroll through the engineering spaces, and a glimpse at the recently patched holes, the boarding party had returned to where they started.

The Imperial was a talkative sort — eager to trade gossip and brag about his trips to Ruusan's surface. And Obota, who knew that such information could come in handy, listened carefully. The two were thick as thieves by the time they passed out through the lock.

The bay was pressurized, so Obota accompanied the lieutenant all the way to the assault shuttle and was already congratulating himself on a job well done when the other officer noticed the *Crow*. He pointed, and Jan, who was watching via the ship's holo cams, felt her blood run cold. The Imperial turned to Obota. "What in the world is *that* thing?"

They had anticipated the question of course, but Obota had expected to hear it earlier and was thrown off balance. He struggled to recover. "Not much to look at is she? We lost our shuttle about three months back, the captain requested a new one, and that's what they gave us."

The lieutenant nodded sympathetically. "Everything is in short supply — which is why the CO is so happy to get his hands on those

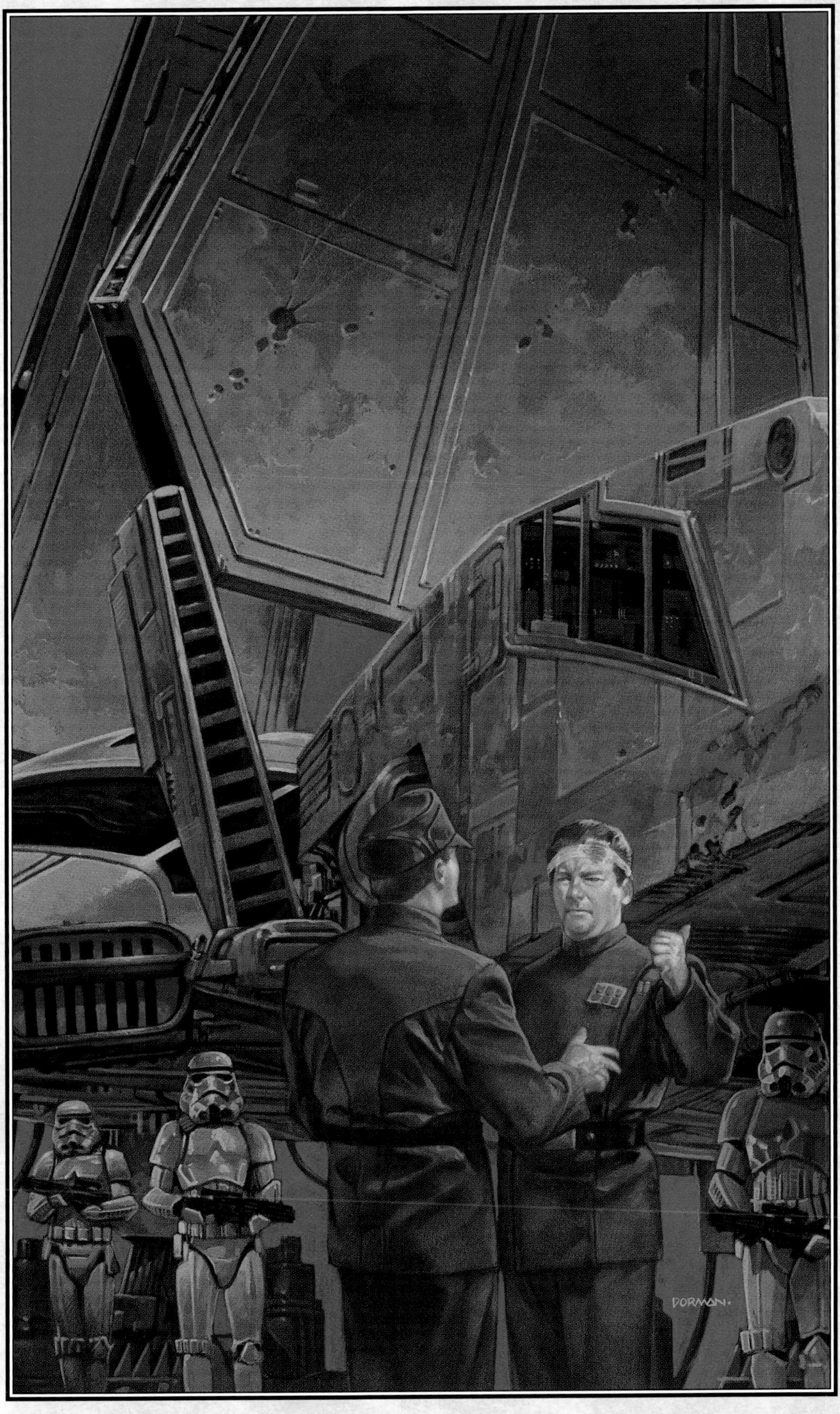
DORMAN.

torpedoes. The Group has half the ordnance it's entitled to, which would hurt during a full-scale battle. Blast! I should take a look — but it's such a nuisance."

Kyle, alerted by Jan and still disguised as a warrant officer, burst onto the deck. "The lighter is alongside, sir! They're ready to land."

The bay was too small to accommodate three vessels all at once, so something had to give. Obota half expected the lieutenant to proceed with his inspection anyway and was relieved when he didn't. "Thanks, captain. I've seen enough. Hope we meet again sometime — and here's wishing you a safe trip home."

Obota couldn't help but like the other man. He shook the lieutenant's hand and entered the lock. Kyle did likewise.

Jan watched the proceedings, gave a sigh of relief, and wished it was over. But no sooner had the air been pumped out of the bay, and the shuttle allowed to depart, than a box-shaped lighter took its place.

The lighter carried two humans and twelve load lifters. The droids didn't require any oxygen, and it was a straight shot to the holds, so Obota left the bay open to space. This had the meritorious effect of speeding the process along while simultaneously isolating the pilots.

The lighter made three trips before the last torpedo had been removed from the transport's holds and it was cleared for departure. The moment the Imperial vessel was gone, Obota signaled his intention to carry out what repairs he could and dispatched the *Crow* on a series of errands. There were parts to pick up, rations to secure, and a "training" mission that allowed the agents to pass over Ruusan's northern hemisphere.

Such activities entailed some risk, but they provided the Rebels with an excellent opportunity to familiarize themselves with the Imperial operation and established the *Crow* within the overall pattern of the Battle Group's comings and goings. The landing, and all that followed, came sixteen hours later.

⇒•◊•⇐

Having received the necessary clearances, the *High Hauler* separated from the Imperial Battle Group and prepared for hyperspace. No one paid much attention to the evolution since it qualified as both routine and boring.

And while the fleet operations officer did make note of the fact that the transport passed through a Class I security zone on its way through the upper reaches of Ruusan's atmosphere, he wrote it off to the commanding officer's lack of experience. Some things are best ignored . . . or so it seemed to him.

Nonetheless, it was during that brief moment when the freighter swept past the planet that the *Moldy Crow* left the security of the larger ship's launch bay and plummeted through the stratosphere. Jan had the controls. She scanned the instrument panel, waited till they were well inside the atmosphere, and fired the drives. "So far, so good."

Kyle nodded. "Yeah, but it won't take them long to make us. We need a place to hide."

"True," the other agent agreed, "but let's check the settlement first . . . the one the lieutenant spoke of."

"Fort Nowhere?"

"Exactly. We could use a guide, someone who knows the surface, and that's the logical place to look."

"Good idea," Kyle agreed, "but quickly, before they sic a wing of TIE fighters on us." Jan nodded and pushed the ship down through a thin layer of clouds.

Wee Gee, the utility droid Kyle's father had designed and the two of them had built, peered over their shoulders. The machine could assume a nearly endless variety of configurations but most often resembled an inverted U. His right arm was the most powerful. It incorporated four articulated joints and a C-shaped grasper. The left was less massive but mounted a human-style tool hand. A repulsorlift engine enabled Wee Gee to hover just off the deck.

The droid made a series of beeping sounds. Kyle nodded his head. "That's right, boy — Ruusan looks a lot different from Sulon."

Wee Gee made a chirruping sound and clamped himself to a bulkhead.

Concerned that they might be detected, Kyle scanned the full spectrum of comm channels. There was some routine chatter, bursts of static as computers exchanged high-speed data packets, and something else, something so weak, so intermittent he wasn't sure it was intentional. Except that it *felt* intentional, and if the Jedi had learned anything over the last few months, it was to trust his feelings.

The ship shuddered as Jan leveled out over an undulating desert and followed the terrain as it rose and fell. *If* they stayed low enough, *if* they were lucky, the agents would escape detection by ground-based sensors.

"Listen to this," Kyle said, turning up the volume. "Does it mean anything to you?"

Jan listened to what sounded like a series of clicks. Some came in rapid succession, while others had short periods of silence between them. "No, but it's repetitive, which would seem to rule out natural phenomena of some sort."

"That's what I thought," Kyle agreed. "Let's try something . . . " He touched some keys, ran the signal through the ship's computer, and waited for a response. A screen came to life, and words appeared and scrolled from top to bottom.

"The signal in question exhibits a ninety-nine-percent match with a primitive code involving two alternating symbols. Specific combinations of these symbols stand in for letters — just as binary notation provides a symbolic representation of words and numbers."

Kyle felt a sense of excitement, demanded a translation, and watched the text appear. "Land fifty-six kilometers due south of Fort Nowhere."

The agent checked to see if there was more, found there wasn't, and pointed to the screen. "Look! There they are!"

"There *who* are?" Jan asked cynically. "The colonists? Or a company of stormtroopers?"

Kyle shrugged. "Anything's possible . . . but it *feels* right."

Jan brought the *Crow* up, cleared a mountain of sand, and watched Kyle from the corner of her eye. She hadn't planned to fall in love with him, or anyone else for that matter, but it had happened and she was stuck with it. Stuck with him *and* his talent. It was as if he had a whole set of additional senses — senses she didn't have.

Jan felt a hand cover hers, turned to meet Kyle's gaze, and saw him smile. "Are you all right?"

The agent thought about it for a second, realized that she was, and gave a nod. "Yes, as long as I have you."

Kyle squeezed her hand. "As if you could get rid of me . . . watch that ridge!"

Jan threw the *Crow* to the right, guided the ship through a U-shaped gap, and both of them laughed.

Kyle had noticed that the signal grew steadily stronger as they approached Fort Nowhere. Then, just as the *Crow* flew over some badly burned ruins, the indicator bar shot upward.

"Let's take another look," Kyle suggested, pointing back over his shoulder. "There could be survivors."

Jan nodded, put the ship into a tight turn, and dumped speed. The settlement, or what was left of it, made a sad sight indeed. There was very little left except for burned-out buildings, tumble-down walls, and blackened earth. A single gra grazed next to the abandoned fort.

Kyle gave a low whistle. "Look at that! Not a building left standing . . . why?"

Jan knew the question was rhetorical and didn't answer. The Imperials had been out to eradicate the settlers or, failing that, to make sure they were reduced to little more than hunter-gatherers.

"All right," Kyle said, "I don't sense any intelligent life forms around here . . . let's try the landing zone."

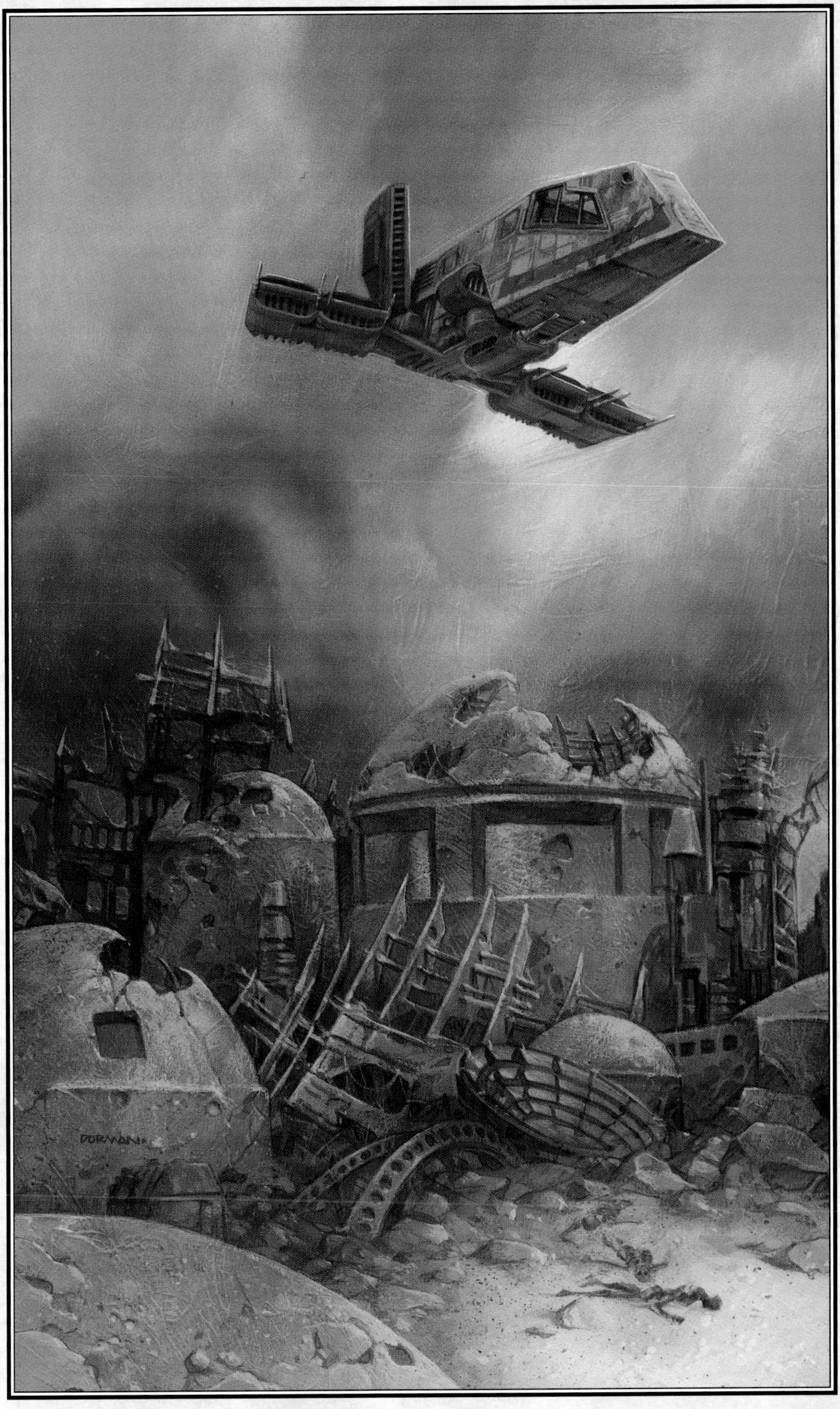
DORMAN

Jan, who still wondered about the wisdom of such a move, turned toward the south. It took less than fifteen minutes to reach their destination. It consisted of a flood plain located between two ancient riverbeds. One thing was for sure, there was very little chance of an ambush, since there was nowhere to hide. Jan banked to starboard. "It looks like nobody's home — what now?"

"Looks can be deceiving," Kyle replied. "Somebody's watching — I can *feel* it."

Jan frowned. "Somebody good? Or somebody bad?"

Kyle shrugged. "Sorry, I can't tell. Let's put her down, keep the weapons systems on-line, and see what happens."

Jan sighed, wished there was another way, and followed Kyle's suggestion. The *Crow* swooped in, hovered for a moment, and settled onto alluvial gravel. Jan left the weapons systems on, set the controls for a hot start, and slaved the sensors to a handheld remote.

It was then and only then that the agent followed her companion outside. He knelt next to the ship and allowed gravel to sift through his fingers. Metal pinged as it cooled, and a breeze swept in from the north. Jan drew the sweet, unrecycled air deep into her lungs. "Nice, isn't it?"

Kyle encountered something solid with his fingers, brushed the gravel away, and broke the object free. "Hey! Look at this!"

He held up the object for her inspection, and Jan saw what remained of an ancient dagger. The handle, which might have been made of wood or bone, had decayed hundreds of years before, but the blade was good as new.

Then, as if sensitized by Kyle's find, her eye fastened onto something protruding from the plain. The Rebel walked over, toed the object with her boot, and felt it give. She bent over, found a grip, and pulled it free. "Look, Kyle! A helmet!"

Kyle stood and moved in her direction. "It looks like we stumbled onto an ancient battlefield . . . I wonder who won?"

The question went unanswered as something whirred over the agent's head. Jan's blaster was halfway out of its holster when Kyle grabbed her arm. "No! Let them look."

The device completed a circuit of the ship and returned. It was shaped like a boomerang and equipped with sensors. Jan had never seen anything quite like it — which seemed to suggest the colonists rather than the Imperials. The machine hovered, as if to examine them, turned, and entered the *Crow*. Wee Gee had remained aboard — and Kyle could imagine the machines examining each other. His thoughts turned to the flyer's owners. "Cautious aren't they?"

Jan nodded. "And with good reason."

The flyer, if that's what the device could properly be called, exited the ship, circled over their heads, and darted toward the west. It returned seconds later, ran through the same sequence again, and accelerated away.

"They want us to follow," Kyle said calmly. "Let's crank her up."

The Rebels reentered the ship, checked their sensors, and lifted off. The remote hovered, zipped out in front of them, and sped away. The boomerang-shaped machine made pretty good time for something its size, but it was difficult to maintain visual contact and to fly that slowly. Jan was relieved when the device lost altitude and prepared to land.

Kyle watched a pair of low-lying hills reach up to embrace them and used his recently developed talent to monitor the Force. It was like an enormous lake, calm for the most part, but responsive to the least disturbance. There were sentients up ahead — a number of them. Were they colonists? Survivors from the attack on Fort Nowhere? Or stormtroopers waiting in ambush? Logic suggested the former — his emotions the latter.

Grif Grawley lay on top of one of two hills that guarded the entrance to the Valley and the ruins beyond. The statue that had occupied the platform off to his left had fallen hundreds of years before. The remains of it were scattered down the forward slope and pointed toward a skillfully sculpted hand. The palm was blackened where signal fires had burned, beckoning travelers from many kilometers away. It must have been something to see. Carole touched his arm. "Grif! Look! Here they come."

The colonist looked, grabbed his electrobinoculars, and looked again. It was a ship sure enough — with Fido in the lead. He grinned. There was no telling who the visitors were, but one thing was for sure, the ship was clean. He had monitored the inspection himself. "What do you think?" Carole inquired. "Are they Rebels?"

Grif tracked the ship as it passed and descended toward the ground. "That's a good question, hon. You saw the video — did you recognize the man?"

"No, I don't think so . . ."

"Well, I could be wrong, but he looked kinda familiar. A lot like Morgan Katarn's boy . . . the one who left Sulon for the Imperial Military Academy. Question is, am I right? And *if* I am, what side is he on? Time to find out." The courtyard was large enough to accommodate a squadron of X-wings. Jan chose a spot between the once-spectacular fountain and the broad flight of stairs that led up and into the temple. A group of humans, all armed, monitored her progress.

The *Crow* landed with a solid thump. The Rebels assigned Wee Gee to keep watch and made their way down the ramp and out into the increasingly warm atmosphere. A man with a three-day growth of beard

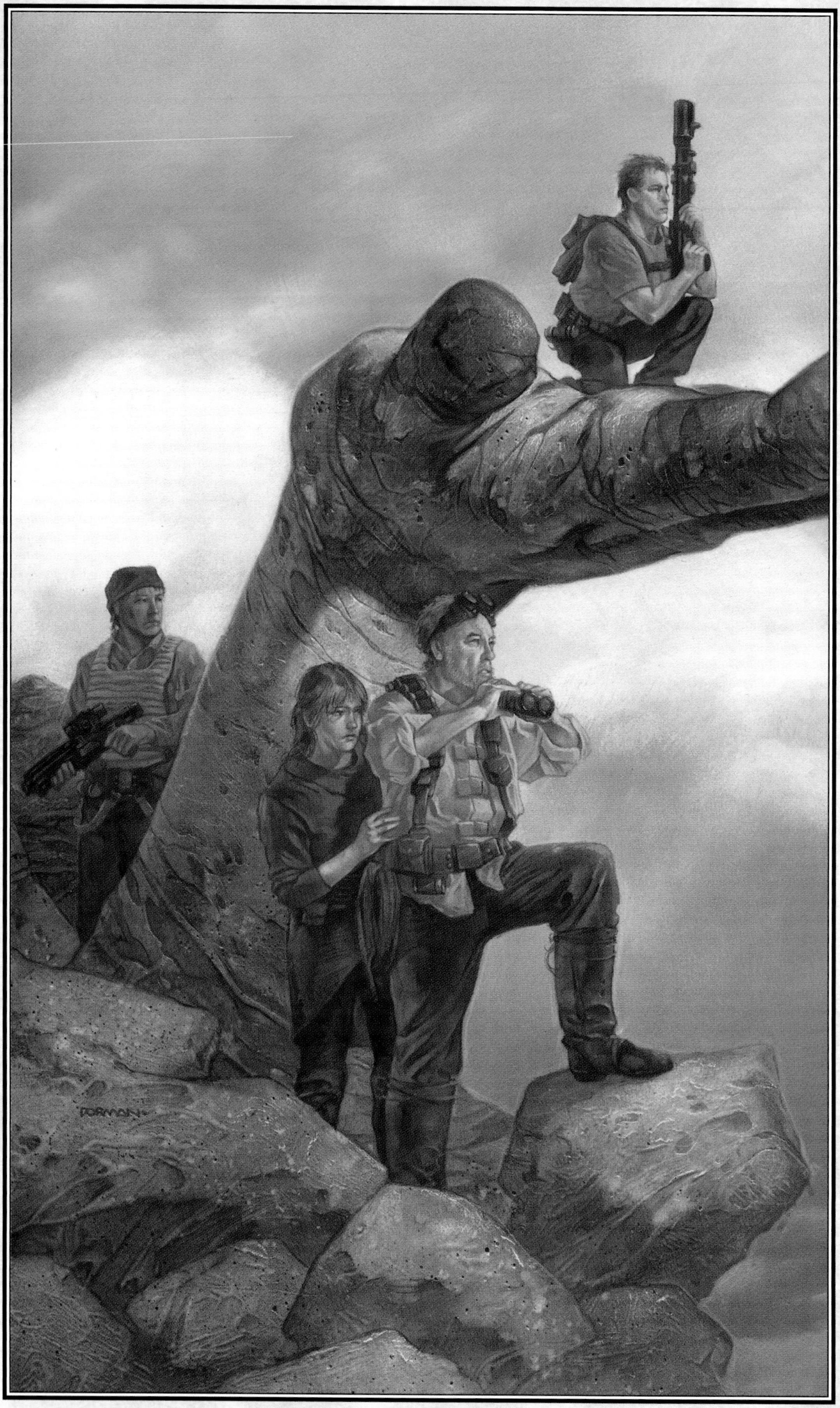

came forward, gave his name as Grif Grawley, and pumped Kyle's hand. "Howdy, son, how's your dad?"

Kyle peered into the other man's face, realized who it was, and grinned. "Citizen Grawley? Is that you? This is wonderful! How's your wife?"

"I'm fine," Carole said, stepping forward. "Thanks to your father . . . We were in trouble back on Sulon and he brought us here."

Grif cleared his throat. "Which raises an interesting question, son. We know which side your dad's on, but you're something of a mystery. Drop the blaster *and* the lightsaber. That goes for you too, young lady . . . till we sort things out."

The agents looked around, saw more than a dozen weapons pointed in their direction, and did as they were told.

"That's better," Grif said equably. "Now, where were we? Oh, yeah, how's your father?"

"Dead," Kyle answered bitterly. "Remember the spaceport? Well, that's where they displayed his head. On a spike for all to see. That's why I'm here, to avenge his death, but more than that, to stop the Imperials from looting the Valley of the Jedi."

Carole Grawley's hand came up to her mouth, and her husband scowled. Morgan Katarn? Dead? It might be a lie . . . but Grif didn't think so. He swore, turned to a group of bystanders, and gave some orders. "Lasko, Kimber, Pardy — throw some netting over that ship and clear the plaza. The Imps aren't blind, you know . . . Come on, you two — let's take it in out of the sun. Cold in the morning and warm later on, that's how it is around here."

The Rebels felt naked without their weapons and more than a little nervous with so many blasters pointed in their direction. Grif led them up the stairs and through an enormous entryway. The temple's interior was surprisingly well lit thanks to an ancient system of skylights and mirrors. A dozen shafts of light, each arriving from a different angle, converged on the likeness of a man. He leaned forward, his chin supported by a fist.

Grif gestured to the space around him. "Welcome to our temporary home. Those fortunate enough to survive the attack on Fort Nowhere banded together, collected what resources they could, and came here."

Carole Grawley listened with amazement as her normally tactless husband papered over the fact that the "townies," as he liked to call them, had ignored his warnings, taken terrible losses, and fled into the badlands. An area about which they knew very little. She would never forget the day they had arrived, setting off the perimeter alarms and interrupting her husband's mid-afternoon nap.

The fact that Grif had agreed to help them, and subsequently metamorphosed into their leader, was no less than a miracle. Or so it seemed to her.

Oblivious to his wife's thoughts, Grif pointed toward a makeshift table and the equipment piled beyond. "Take a load off and tell us the story. Most things happen at night around here . . . so we have plenty of time."

Kyle took a seat and tried to ignore the onlookers. He told the story of how he had gone to the Academy, received the news of his father's death, and headed for home. It was during the journey that he met Jan for the second time, learned that his father had been murdered by the Empire, and swore himself to the Rebel cause.

The raid on Danuta didn't seem relevant, so he left that out and went straight to events on Sulon. These were of considerable interest to most of those present, since that's where most of them came from and, in many cases, hoped to return.

Kyle described his battles with Yun, Gorc, Pic, and 8t88 in dry, dispassionate terms, explained how Jan and he had recovered the necessary coordinates, and why they had come.

A settler named Lasko, the same one who had been brought to his knees by Sariss, listened with interest. Could the Jedi in Katarn's story be the same ones who destroyed Fort Nowhere? It certainly sounded that way.

Jan felt it was a story well told — but at least one of those present disagreed. He was a pugnacious individual with an underthrust jaw and massive shoulders. His name was Pardy, Luther Pardy, and he wore Kyle's weapons as if they were his. "It makes a nice story, boy, a *real* nice story, kind o' like the fairy tales the missus tells the young'uns. Why should we believe this dreck? 'Specially the stuff about the Force, Jedi Knights, and all that. Sounds kind o' convenient to me — sort of like what a spy would say."

Lasko eyed both men, decided to support Katarn if it came to that, and allowed a hand to rest on his blaster.

A cloud passed in front of the sun. The light level dropped by twenty percent. The statue seemed to frown, and all eyes turned toward Kyle. Slowly, so as not to startle one of the trigger-happy colonists, he stood.

Pardy, who outweighed the agent by a good thirty pounds, grinned. A quick, easy victory would raise his status within the group. Make Grawley listen more. He licked his lips.

Kyle met the other man's eyes, extended his hand as if ready to shake, and visualized what he wanted. An object whirred through the air, slapped the surface of his palm, and made a popping noise. Energy sizzled as the lightsaber came to life, and Pardy stepped back. A half-dozen blasters came up but fell when Grif shook his head. "Well, Pardy, no more questions? I didn't think so. Guess you'd better return that blaster. Welcome to Ruusan, kid — and you too, Jan. Tell us about that Valley and what we can do to help."

Lasko felt a tremendous sense of relief. Only a Jedi could defeat a Jedi. Now there was hope.

———————>>·0·<<———————

There was no especially safe time to move around the planet's surface, but night offered some protection and was the only time when the bouncers ventured out. It had been Grif's idea to meet with the locals and seek their counsel. After all, the bouncers were either native to Ruusan or had been there so long that it didn't make much difference, and they knew the planet better than anyone.

Grif nudged the agent's arm. The two of them, plus Jan and six of the most able-bodied colonists, had taken refuge in a fortress of stone. A boulder lay at the center of the refuge, surrounded by the tumble of smaller rocks to which it had inadvertently given birth. Carved from their parent's flanks by the combined forces of heat, water, and cold, the offspring provided a vantage point from which the Rebels could watch the surrounding plain.

Ruusan had no less than three moons — all of which were visible. Grif pointed to the flat area in front of them. "That's where the bouncers are most likely to appear . . . They're shaped like balls, have retractable tentacles, and rely on the wind for propulsion. All of which might explain their lifestyle, patience, and inherent fatalism."

Kyle raised an eyebrow, and Grif looked self-conscious. "Hey, it makes sense, doesn't it? You don't need no degree in anthropology to figure that out."

"It makes a lot of sense. Go on."

"Well, they have big eyes, for gathering light, and love to roll in front of the wind. That's when they look for obstacles, steer for them, and bounce into the air."

"Hence the name 'bouncers,' " Kyle put in.

"Right," Grif confirmed. "And that's when they float — as far as the wind will carry them."

"They sound wonderful," Jan said wistfully. "I hope they come."

"There's no way to be sure," the colonist replied, "but the conditions are right. Your father knew them," Grif added, turning toward Kyle. "And they still talk about him, or write about him, since that's how they communicate."

"The bouncers knew my father?" Kyle asked incredulously. "How could that be?"

"Your dad was an interesting man," the settler replied. "Once he put us on the ground and got things organized, he borrowed a skimmer and took off. Everybody said he was crazy. Who knows when he ran into the bouncers, but he did. They call him 'the knight who never was,' whatever that means."

Kyle felt goose bumps ripple the length of his arms. His father could have been a Jedi Knight . . . and chose not to. That was *his* theory anyway, which echoed what the bouncers said. But how could they know?

"Look!" Jan said excitedly. "I see some white blobs!"

"Here they come," Grif confirmed, peering through his electrobinoculars. "Watch closely . . . you're in for a treat."

The creatures sent ripples through the Force. Kyle had raised his electrobinoculars and was about to take a look when another presence registered on his consciousness.

The agent turned, scrambled onto a flat-topped rock, and scanned the southern horizon. It took less than five seconds to acquire the incoming targets and identify them for what they were: a skimmer with two speeder bikes as escorts. "Grif! Jan! We've got company. Alert the others."

"What about the bouncers?" Jan demanded. "We've got to warn them!"

Kyle turned, realized the globes were much closer than they had been, and watched them bounce high into the air. His mind was racing, trying to come up with a solution, when the speeder bikes opened fire.

Smaller and therefore faster than the heavily laden skimmer, they split the rock pile between them, turned, and went in opposite directions. One toward the west and one toward the east. The light generated by their energy cannon split the night into geometric shapes and was lost in the distance. The bouncers reacted by turning inward.

"They're clustering together," Grif called out, "so the troopers on the skimmer can slaughter them!"

"Not tonight they won't," Jan said grimly, "not while I'm alive."

The agent took her blast rifle, scrambled up onto an even higher perch, and wrapped the sling around her elbow. Kyle considered trying to stop her and knew it was useless. Jan was going to war in spite of the fact that a fire fight was likely to reveal their presence and threaten an already perilous mission. All for some aliens she hadn't even met. Mon Mothma would never approve. Still, Kyle loved her for it and turned to Grif. "If your people want to even the score, here's their chance. Prisoners are fine . . . but nobody gets away . . . *nobody*."

Jan wanted to take full advantage of surprise. That meant that each of the first shots had to count. She peered into the scope, led the speeder bike by what she judged to be the right distance, and touched the trigger.

Coherent energy burped outward, the Imperial ran into it, and the bike exploded. Still-flaming debris rained down as the surviving rider fired into the rocks and called for help.

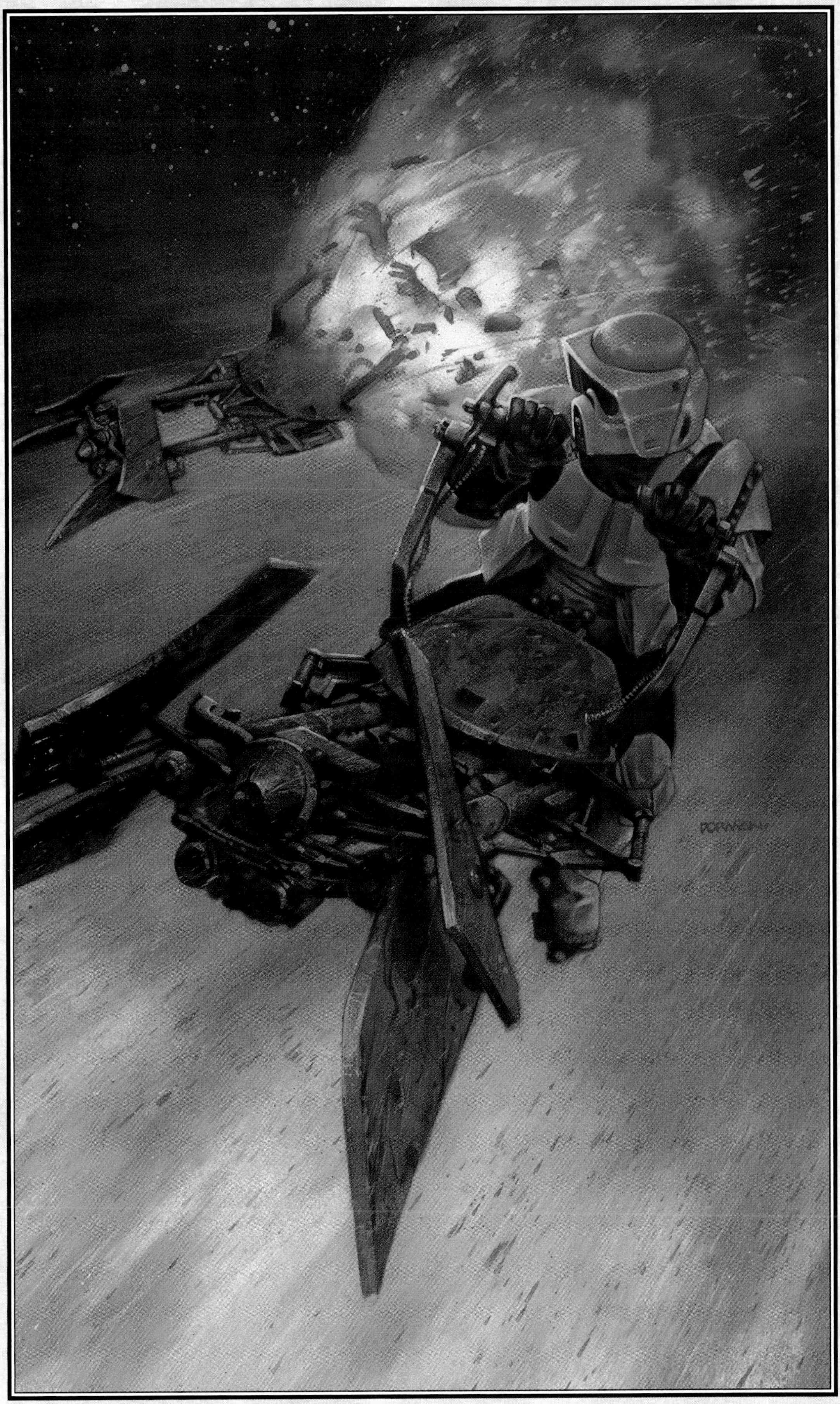

The officer in charge of the patrol, a Lieutenant Aagon, saw the explosion, knew his stormtroopers would be less vulnerable on the ground, and ordered the helmsman to land. The troopers bailed out, Aagon followed, and they ran for the rocks. It was a short sprint and easily done.

The officer knew the Rebs were on the opposite side of the rocks and wanted to keep them there. His helmsman, a sergeant named Forley, and the gunner, a rating named Leeno, were still aboard. Aagon spoke into his comm.

"Take the skimmer around to the other side of the rocks. Pin down the Rebels. We'll attack from behind."

The dead biker had been Forley's best friend. He planned to do more than pin down the Rebs — he planned to kill them. "Sir! Yes, sir!"

Confident of Forley's competence, Aagon led six troopers into the rocky maze. He could have called for reinforcements — but had some good reasons not to.

The first related to the fact that his authorized patrol area lay ten klicks to the south. A nice enough collection of ravines and gullies but not the sort of place the bouncers were likely to go, which meant the hunting was poor.

The second reason had to do with his immediate superior, an ambitious sort who would just as soon take all the credit and let Aagon do all the fighting.

No, the lieutenant decided, we'll kill the Rebels, report the engagement as taking place twelve klicks to the south, and score some points in the next dispatch. Just the thing to fuel his next promotion.

Confident that his plan would work and eager to get on with it, the officer scrambled over a boulder and slipped through a gap. The troopers followed.

⟫◦⟪

The skimmer rounded the rocks and, with support from the remaining bike, opened fire. There were lots of places to hide, so the attack had very little effect. But Forley knew a thing or two and changed his tactics. He ordered Leeno to concentrate his fire on a single boulder. The gunner did so, watched the rock start to glow, and was soon rewarded with an explosion.

Kyle ducked as razor-sharp rock fragments flew in every direction, took one Rebel's arm off, and exploded as they hit the surrounding boulders. The man started to scream then stopped as another piece of shrapnel hit him in the head. Kyle scuttled over to Jan. "Give me a two-minute lead and take them out."

Jan nodded grimly and wasn't the least bit disturbed when Kyle took most of the Rebel force with him. He had led stormtroopers into battle himself, and successfully, too.

A teenage girl had been left to watch Jan's back. The girl's name was Portia. She had dark skin, white teeth, and intelligent eyes. The agent took a potshot at the speeder bike, gestured to the girl, and followed her through the rocks.

Light flashed behind them. The women paused and looked back. Another rock had started to glow, so they ducked behind a ledge. Jan eyed the teenager's weapon. It appeared to be clean and well cared for. The rock exploded, fragments rattled off the surrounding surfaces, and the Rebels ignored them. "So, Portia, are you any good with that thing?"

"One of the best," the teenager answered confidently. "That's what they tell me anyway."

"Good," Jan answered tightly, "because we're about to bet *my* life on it."

———○———

Trooper RW957 was where he liked to be, at the tail end of the column, bringing up the rear. A position where he was less likely to be killed in an ambush, sent forward on some suicidal mission, or accidentally shot in the back. Yes, sir, RW957 thought to himself, you've gotta have a plan if you want to survive, and not just *one* plan, but a whole lotta plans, that's why . . .

The only warning was the whisper of fabric. An arm slid around the trooper's neck, a hand pulled off his helmet, and moonlight reflected off the blade. The stormtrooper thought the word "help" but never had an opportunity to actually say it.

———○———

Jan climbed up onto a carefully chosen rock, lit the flare, and waved it in the air. The trooper on the speeder bike took the bait, turned toward the target, and fired his braking jets. "A steady platform makes for an accurate shot . . . " That's what the manual said, and the manual was right.

Portia forced herself to wait until the target was square into her sight, squeezed the trigger just the way you were supposed to, and held it down. The first few bolts were deflected by the dull-white armor, but the fourth managed to scorch it, and the fifth, sixth, and seventh drilled on through. The trooper fell out of his saddle, the bike began to drift, and Jan threw the flare as far as she could.

———○———

Aagon heard the rock explosions, saw the flare go off, and wondered what the Rebs were up to. The officer felt for a handhold, found what he was looking for, and pulled himself up. The top of the rock was flat and sloped toward the north. Something moved, and he raised his blaster. That's when a finger poked his shoulder. "I wouldn't do that if I were you . . . drop it."

The Imperial was in the process of turning, of trying to kill the man behind him, when he heard something "pop." He blinked as a bar of incandescent light appeared, grew momentarily smaller, and flashed down toward his face. There was time for one last thought, something profound would have been nice, but nothing came. The light was the brightest thing Aagon had ever seen.

The skimmer had fired countless bolts of energy and all to no avail. It hovered as Forley struggled to make a decision — not something the Imperial command structure trained sergeants to do. Both bike riders were dead, and he couldn't raise the lieutenant. The whole thing should be over by now. What to do? Stay? Or run? Neither alternative seemed very attractive. The skimmer made a highly visible target, but running entailed problems of its own. What if Aagon and the rest of the squad were alive? And how would he explain where they'd been? The whole thing was a mess.

Leeno interrupted Forley's thoughts. "Sarge! Behind you!"

Forley turned, realized that a large white globe had drifted to within centimeters of his face, and threw up his hands. The bouncer used its tentacles to grab hold of them, pulled itself in, and enveloped the sergeant's head.

Horrified, Leeno swiveled his weapon toward the stern and opened fire. The bouncer died, but so did Forley, which caused the Imperial to panic. He jumped over the side and ran. The gunner was still running when the bouncers drifted down out of the sky, knocked him to his knees, and pinned him down. Grif, along with a couple of Rebels, arrived two minutes later. Leeno, his mind filled with images of the way Forley had died, continued to scream.

The three sisters had fled the sky, the stars were barely visible, and a jagged pink line marked the eastern horizon. Hours had passed while the Rebels buried the dead, camouflaged the graves, and loaded weapons

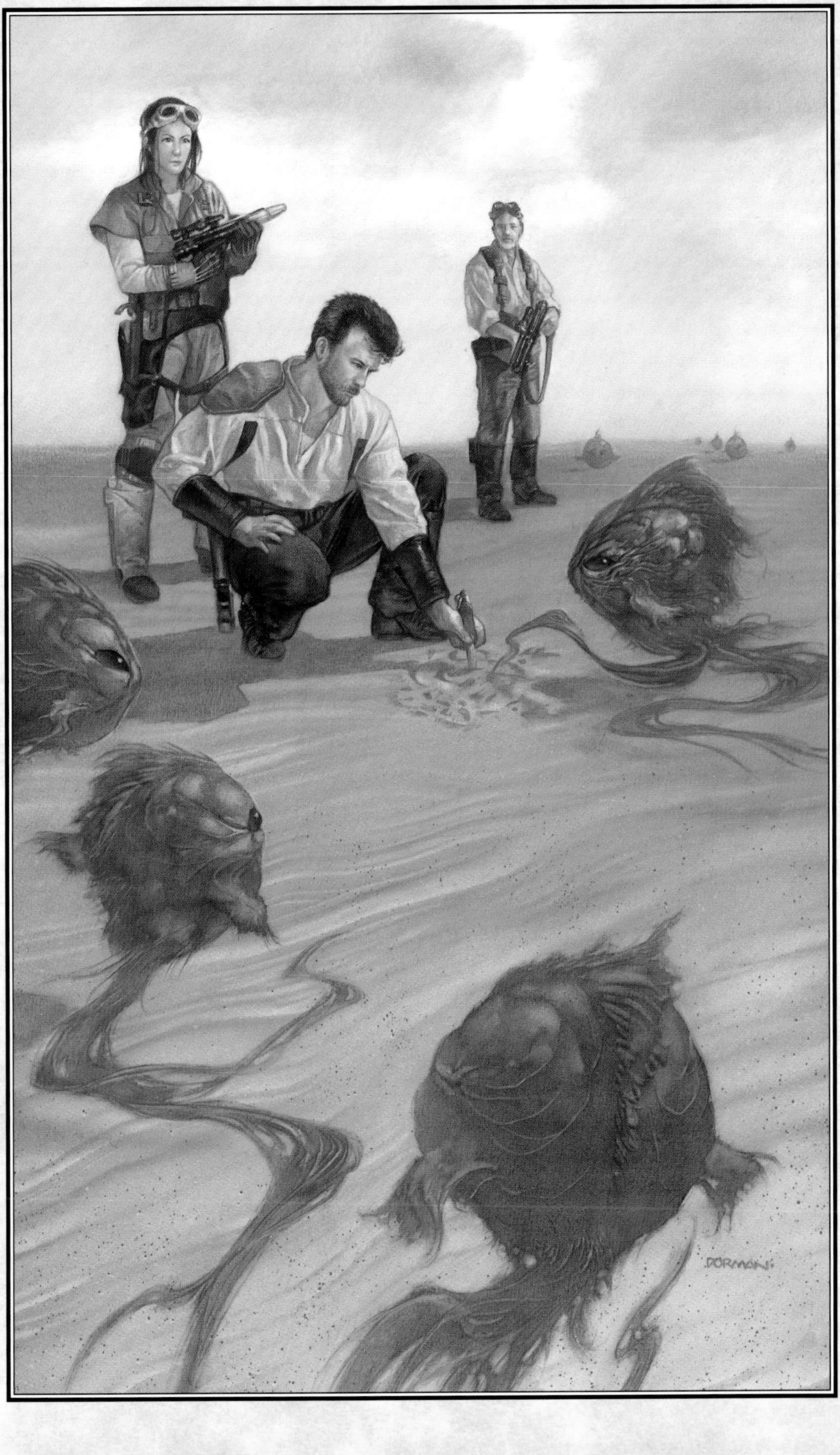
DORMAN

and other gear onto the Imperial skimmer. "A nice piece of equipment," Grif said, patting a sturdy flank. "We can use it."

"*And* the speeder bike," Jan put in, "not to mention the other stuff."

"Some of which may still be out there," Kyle said, remembering how difficult it had been to search in the dark. "I hope the wrong people don't find it."

Grif shrugged. "What are the odds? Besides, we've gotta get out of here before the sun comes up and the search begins."

The words made sense. Kyle turned toward the delegation of bouncers. Their skin fluttered as they leaned into the oncoming breeze and used their tentacles as anchors.

One of the band, an individual Grif referred to as "Floater," had agreed to serve as a guide. He moved among his peers and touched each one of them good-bye.

Their leader, an especially leathery specimen who had met Morgan Katarn during his visit to the planet, watched as Kyle scratched words into the hardpan with a combat knife. "You and your people must hide . . . will you be all right?"

The tentacle felt dry and warm where it touched the agent's hand, slid downward, and took control of the knife. The syntax was strange but understandable. "Blowing wind steady. All right will be."

Kyle accepted the knife and carved a reply. "I am sorry about the death of your friend-mate. Thank you for allowing Floater to help us."

"Sorry are we at the death of your race-person," the bouncer replied. "Floater goes where he must — though death it may bring."

Kyle thought about Jerec, about those who served him, and felt an emptiness at the pit of his stomach. He took the knife. "You know what we came to do . . . will we succeed?"

The bouncer blinked. The blade grated on tiny bits of rock as it carved words into the soil. "Everyone knows that a knight shall come, that a battle will be fought, and the prisoners will go free. If not now . . . then someday."

The answer was far from satisfying — and the words echoed long after the wind had erased them.

CHAPTER 4

Yun had kicked the covers off his bunk. They lay bunched on the deck. His limbs twitched in reaction to the horror of what he was about to do. The rain splashed onto the already saturated ground. A layer of what looked like mist or ectoplasm hovered over the well-churned mud. Twenty men and women knelt before an open grave. They were guilty of something — he couldn't remember what.

A few prisoners had tears streaming down their cheeks, others snarled their defiance, but most bore no expressions at all. They simply stared into the trench and awaited their fates.

Yun hefted the lightsaber over his head, felt it grow heavier, and realized it had been transformed into an old-fashioned sword. The curved blade had a razor-sharp edge. That's when the Jedi remembered that he had dreamed this dream many times before. He struggled to wake himself, was unable to do so, and knew what would happen.

For perhaps the thousandth time, the face of Nij Por Ral, a somewhat portly professor of linguistics looked up at him and begged for mercy. "Please! I beg of you, spare us!"

One aspect of Yun's personality felt no particular animosity toward the man and wanted to grant his request, but another part, the shadow that dwelt within, hungered for status and recognition. Status and recognition that could and would be granted by Jerec and Sariss *if* he lived up to their expectations.

Gleaming steel began its downward course. Yun regretted the blow even as it fell. Not because of the injury it would cause, but because it was flawed, and everyone would know it. He winced as the blade sank into Por Ral's shoulder. Metal grated on bone as the linguist bellowed in pain and Yun struggled to pull his weapon free. Finally, having wiggled the sword back and forth, the sword came loose. Sick with shame, the Jedi put an end to the prisoner's anguished screams.

But the horror wasn't over — not by a long shot. Yun moved down the row. His mother, father, and sister knelt before him. They beseeched him with their eyes, but to no avail. He had already cut them down, if not with steel, then with words. But no matter how many times he killed them, they always came back.

The blade rose and fell. Heads rolled, tumbled into the ditch, and were followed by the bodies to which they belonged. The rain, combined with the blood of his victims, had soaked through the Jedi's clothes. He shivered, struggled to raise the sword, and was surprised by its weight. It was heavy, *too* heavy, as if each life had somehow added to its mass . . .

Light flooded the compartment, and Yun jerked in response. The Jedi rolled off the bed, activated his lightsaber, and rose ready to fight. Boc, who stood in the hatch, laughed mockingly. "What's the matter, boy? A little nervous, are we? Well, pull yourself together. It seems Jerec has need of your scrawny presence."

Yun took a step forward, lightsaber in hand, but the other Jedi laughed. "Save your energy, boy . . . it's my guess you're going to need it."

The already Spartan cabin looked even more bare as Jerec placed the last of his meager belongings into the case. While the Jedi had no interest in quantity, he was choosy about the possessions he had and didn't like others to touch them.

There was a knock at the door. The way each person interacted with the Force was unique, and this disturbance was typical of Yun. A promising student — but filled with self-doubt. Ah well, Jerec thought to himself, a bit of seasoning will fix that. "Enter."

Yun entered cautiously, wondered what the older Jedi had in store for him, and hoped the Master was in a good mood. Jerec nodded to acknowledge Yun's presence. "Thank you for coming . . . I need your assistance."

Jerec needed his help! The younger Jedi felt his heart swell to at least twice its normal size. He couldn't wait to tell Sariss. "Yes, my lord, how can I help?"

"Phase two of the survey is now complete. The tower is in the final stages of construction. That being the case, the *real* work can begin. I leave for the surface in an hour."

Yun nodded. "Yes, my lord."

"Have you studied the survey results?"

"Yes, my lord."

"And the key findings were?"

"A large valley, filled with thousands of Jedi graves, and invested with their power."

"*And?*"

Yun shrugged. "And satellite caves, some empty, some filled with potentially valuable artifacts."

"Potentially *valuable* artifacts," Jerec emphasized, closing the valise. "Just the thing to help defray the cost of this fleet — and keep the Imperial nitpickers off my back. Blast, but they're stupid! The entire universe spread before them and they see none of it. Still, they are what they are, and we must accept that. Loot, that's what they want, and loot they shall have. Thanks to you."

Yun felt his heart sink. Loot? Junk was more like it — interesting junk but junk nevertheless. Especially when compared to the main chamber and the unimaginable power available there. But thinking such thoughts and expressing them were two different things. Yun swallowed his disappointment. "Yes, my lord. How should I proceed?"

Jerec turned his empty sockets in Yun's direction. "Accompany me to the surface, locate an officer named Vig, and assume command. The work proceeds slowly — too slowly — and I want you to correct that."

Yun sensed a trap, gathered his courage, and asked the obvious question. "I've met Major Vig. He seems capable enough . . . so what's the problem?"

Jerec smiled. "More than a thousand Jedi spirits are trapped within the Valley's walls — and our efforts stirred them up. Some of the prisoners have taken to howling through corridors, scaring stormtroopers, and creating havoc. The major is beside himself."

Yun cursed his luck. Babysitting spirits and stormtroopers . . . a low-level assignment. Why not Maw? Or Boc? Because Maw was unpredictable — and Boc too cunning. And Sariss? No, Jerec had other more important duties for his second in command to carry out. Yun sighed. "Yes, my lord. I'll pack and join you in the launch bay."

Jerec waited for the hatch to close, felt the younger Jedi's energy start to fade, and smiled. Even the best of blades should be tested.

Yun packed quickly and headed toward the launch bay. He rarely had the chance to spend time with the Master, and he tried to make the most of every opportunity, no matter how brief.

The two men ran into each other in the main corridor — and walked shoulder to shoulder toward the launch bay. Stormtroopers jumped to get out of the way, officers came to attention, while Yun basked in the reflected glory. It was at moments like this that his doubts disappeared and the price seemed worth paying.

The shuttle was waiting, the bay door opened, and a pair of TIE fighters escorted them down. The trip to the surface was uneventful, for which Yun was thankful. Jerec had many unpleasant qualities, but there were exceptions — he could be very charming when he chose to be. The Master regaled Yun with amusing stories, the younger Jedi laughed in all the right places, and the trip was soon over. Jerec made a point of saying good-bye — and the resulting sense of significance followed Yun all the way to his quarters.

⇒▸◦◂⇐

The alarm buzzed and wouldn't stop. Yun reached for the bedside console and discovered that the room's recently installed heating module was on the blink. The Jedi was still in bed when a droid entered the room, announced itself in loud, cheery tones, and placed a tray on the table. "Good morning, sir. Here's your breakfast . . . Is there anything else I can do for you?"

"Yeah, pump some heat in here," Yun growled as he rolled out of bed. "It's freezing."

"Of course, sir, right away, sir," the droid said, making for the door. "I'll send a maintenance droid."

Yun slipped into the fresher and treated himself to a hot, steamy shower. After that, it was a simple matter to slip into some fresh clothes, consume his lukewarm breakfast, and head for work. A stormtrooper had been assigned to guide him and stood at the tower's base. "Good morning, sir. Major Vig sent me . . . I'll lead the way."

The stormtrooper set off, and Yun followed. The ground in front of the tower was crisscrossed with tread marks, supplies sat piled on floater pallets, and security was tight. Even more noticeable, to him at least, was the way the place *felt*.

Each Jedi perceived the Force in his or her own slightly subjective manner. For Yun, it manifested as an eternal hum — a gentle vibration that never went away. But this place was different. The Force felt more intense here, as if it had been amplified, and growled like a ravenous beast. In fact, the activity was *so* strong it could be perceived by those with little or no talent.

They had just entered a ravine and started down a flight of water-eroded stairs, when a banshee-like entity screamed by the stormtrooper's

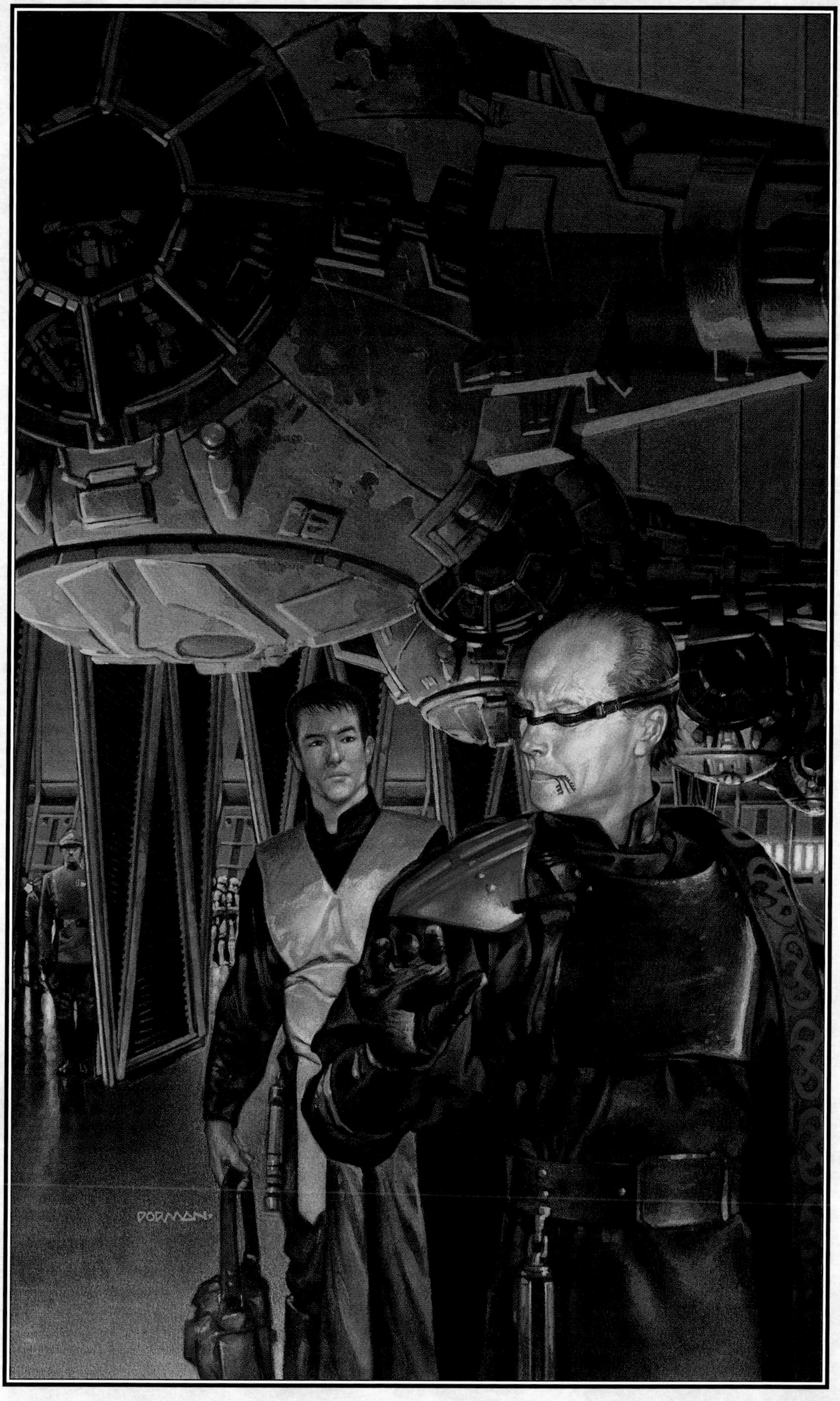
DORMAN

head. The soldier flinched, managed to retain his composure, and turned toward Yun. "They're starting early today, sir. Looks like a rough one."

Given the fact that the Force was more concentrated than usual, Yun found that it was easy to shape a thought and hurl it at the obnoxious spirit. The results were dramatic, to say the least. Angered rather than frightened, the entity summoned even more spirits to the site and sent them howling around the Jedi's head. The trooper, his mind reeling under the assault, broke and ran.

Yun, relying on his training, stood his ground. A voice spoke within his head. "Pain means nothing to such as these. They have suffered for thousands of years. Imagine their plight, understand the horror of it, and communicate that understanding."

The personality associated with the voice seemed familiar somehow, and the Jedi struggled to place it. "Who are you?" Yun demanded. "One of them?"

"No, not really," the voice answered. "I gave you the key . . . try it."

Knowing that both Jerec and Sariss expected him to succeed, not to mention the troopers in the chamber below, Yun followed the instructions. He thought about the spirits who wailed around him, about the extent to which they had suffered, and his anger melted away. He felt a sense of empathy, of understanding, and extended it to those around him.

The change was almost instantaneous. The moaning stopped, the entities slipped away, and the Force grew more tranquil.

Pleased with the results and confident of his ability to deal with similar situations, Yun sent a message of appreciation. "Thank you."

There was no answer from his invisible benefactor — just a momentary sense of warmth.

The stormtrooper had yet to reappear, but Yun had no difficulty following the path downward, past a wall inscribed with ancient hieroglyphics and a spot where a deactivated droid stared into a looted alcove. One of the machine's arms had been converted to a directional sign. Yun took a right.

The side corridor was relatively short and opened into a large chamber. Stand-mounted floods threw light onto the walls, cargo modules stood in untidy piles, and a confrontation was underway.

Major Vig was a big man, with short red hair and a handlebar mustache. It was nonreg, and a constant source of frustration to his superiors, but ultimately tolerated because of his courage and almost legendary competence. Competence that translated to respect — and explained why the stormtroopers were hesitant to ignore both his orders and the blaster in his hand. The officer's voice boomed through the cavern. "Hold it right there . . . the first man to move dies."

There was a moment of silence while the troopers absorbed the officer's words and considered the consequences of what they were about to do. That's when a group of three screamers entered the chamber through the rear wall, passed through the middle of a trooper's chest, and dove through the floor.

It was too much. Eyes bulged in their sockets, heads swiveled in every direction, and the mob moved forward. That's when Yun spoke. "Good morning, gentlemen. I see you're already hard at work! Lord Jerec will be pleased. Sorry about the somewhat unusual working conditions . . . perhaps I can help."

In spite of the fact that very few of the soldiers had ever *seen* Jerec, much less met him, they were well aware of *who* he was and the much exaggerated powers ascribed not only to him, but to the coterie of Jedi who attended him. That being the case, the sudden and unheralded appearance of one such exalted creature took on seemingly mystical qualities. The upshot was that when Yun said he could help, the troopers believed him.

Sensing the change, and correctly interpreting the embarrassed looks that had appeared on his subordinates' faces, Major Vig holstered his side arm. He started to say something, realized Yun was distracted, and waited for the Jedi to take notice. It didn't take very long. Yun completed his interaction with some unseen spirits and smiled.

"I think the matter is resolved — for the moment anyway. Inform your men that while such incidents will no doubt continue, I'll be here to deal with them. That means they can return to work. Lord Jerec has a personal interest in this effort — and there's no time to waste."

Major Vig spoke to his officers, who soon had the troops back at work. Most of his peers would have pressed charges on the theory that a few highly visible executions were a boon to discipline, but Vig didn't blame the troops for being frightened and decided to ignore what they had done. A strategy Yun found interesting.

Sariss, like *her* mentor, had taught Yun that the sort of leadership Vig demonstrated was a sign of weakness and that respect flows from fear. Fear born of power, which was the point of the entire exercise on Ruusan. The major interrupted his thoughts. "Thank you, sir. The screamers have been a constant problem."

Yun shrugged. "Glad I could help. In fact, it looks as if you're stuck with me."

Vig's mustache twitched over what might have been a smile. He knew Yun would be in command but saw that as a plus. The Jedi was welcome to the screamers *and* Jerec, as far as the officer was concerned. "Welcome aboard, sir. Would you like a tour?"

Yun indicated that he would and followed the officer across the main chamber and into one of the many storerooms that branched off from it. The narration had a canned quality suggesting that Vig had given the tour before. "The main chamber is a natural phenomenon, formed by an ancient river, but the storerooms, while still very old, are a good deal more recent. They were carved from solid rock." The officer paused and pointed at a wall. "Look, you can still see the tool marks."

Yun looked, confirmed Vig's observation, and followed the officer into a half-empty room. A droid was hard at work stripping goo off a wall. "Looks weird, doesn't it?" the officer inquired. "Still, the ancients knew what they were doing. They brought down supplies, stacked them along the walls, and sprayed preservative on them. Interestingly enough, the sealer is so much better than what we use for the same purpose that it might be worth duplicating. Here, look at this . . . " Vig sidestepped the droid, took one of the recently freed packages, and placed it in the Jedi's hands.

Yun accepted the object, peeled the last bits of malleable gel off the bottom of the box, and turned it over. It was made of plastic or something very similar. The top featured a single cluster of hieroglyphics and a slightly raised panel. "What is it?"

"Press the panel three times," the officer said mischievously. "Place it on the floor and watch."

Yun did as instructed and stepped back. Ten seconds passed before anything happened. Then, just as the Jedi was about to lose interest, the lid popped open, steam billowed into the room, and a yeasty odor filled the air.

"Lunch!" Vig said delightedly, "or breakfast or dinner as the case may be. Look inside."

The Jedi looked. The box contained fifteen or twenty grub-like things. They wiggled and squirmed with such vigor that the thick, brown sauce lapped the edges of the container.

"We aren't sure which species these meals were prepared for," the officer continued, "and it doesn't really matter. Self-heating rations have been around for a long time — but not ones in which the seemingly inert contents are somehow brought back to life. And what about the heat source? The heat mods in our field rations have a shelf life of about twenty years. These have been sitting around for a thousand or more."

Yun saw the value and understood the means by which Jerec had secured a small fleet with which to pursue his personal ambitions. It was wonderful or horrible, depending on how you chose to view it.

"And that's not all," Vig continued. "Come on . . . wait till you see the rest!"

The Jedi followed the officer into a succession of storerooms where even more treasures were revealed. There was a tractor beam projector no bigger than a wand, healing machines only slightly less effective than bacta tanks, and a fusion reactor so small it could be carried in a backpack. All of which would endear Jerec to his corporate sponsors. A political dynamic that Yun had never considered before.

It was a relatively pleasant morning, interrupted by no more than three screamers, none of whom presented much of a problem.

Yun had lunch with Major Vig, a captain, and two lieutenants in a recently cleared storeroom. They sat at a table complete with white linen, regimental silver, and a freshly prepared meal. A droid served as waiter. Everything went well until the plates were cleared and the atmosphere inexplicably changed.

The first sign that something was wrong was when Lieutenant Hab said something unintelligible, grabbed his throat, and toppled over backward.

A split second passed while the Jedi wondered if Hab had choked on a piece of meat — followed by the realization that the problem was even more serious. Yun struggled to remain calm, fought the temptation to meet force with force, and attempted to reach out.

The entity sensed the movement and released Hab in order to refocus its energies. The spirit seized the tendril of being that linked Yun to his physical body. The Jedi felt a tug — followed by sustained pressure. The entity was trying to pull him out!

The Jedi attempted to withdraw and discovered that he wasn't able to do so. The other entity's hold was too strong. Fear clutched his belly, his mouth opened, and nothing emerged. It was at the very height of his fear that the voice spoke within. "Don't surrender to doubt, my son. Use the same technique you learned earlier. He's stronger, that's all. Even Jedi Masters can lose their sanity after a thousand years of confinement. Anchor your mind, reach out, and understand. The Force will protect you."

Yun swallowed, was glad to discover that he had that much control, and took the risk. Rather than continue his efforts to withdraw, he pushed outward. The entity sensed victory and rushed in. Yun welcomed the spirit, not into his body, but into the warmth of his understanding and the hope of freedom. The ancient was too far gone to be healed, not by a mind so junior, but allowed itself to be soothed.

"Good," the voice said. "You did all anyone could do. He returns to his tomb."

"Who are you?" Yun demanded. "Should I know you?"

"Yes," the voice replied calmly. "You should. For you participated in my murder, and I inhabit your dreams."

"Nij Por Ral?"

"No, though my death followed his."

"Rahn!"

Yun remembered him well. A Jedi who had heard of the Valley and dedicated his life to finding it. Rahn and a group of his associates had been intercepted before they could locate the Valley, and it was Yun's participation in the murders that followed, mixed with other aspects of his life, that still haunted his dreams. The voice was matter-of-fact. "So, you remember."

"Yes."

"Good."

"Why? Why help me?"

"The light within you flickers," the voice answered calmly, "but it continues to burn. The fate of billions upon billions of beings rests on what will happen here. You will play a part."

"A part?" Yun asked, "What kind of part?"

"That," Rahn responded, "is entirely up to you."

Yun felt the connection break, opened his eyes to a room filled with staring faces, and felt very much alone.

Yun wandered the subterranean passageways for the next couple of days, dealt with the occasional screamer, and wished something interesting would happen. It wasn't long before his wish came true.

The Jedi had just left the main corridor, sidestepped a train of heavily laden grav pallets, and was about to enter the third chamber when everything started to shake. Little bits of rock rained down on his head, the dust made him cough, and the floor shook as something heavy hit it. The screams started just as the shaking stopped.

The Jedi could have headed for the surface and knew it was the smart thing to do, but he discovered that his feet had minds of their own. They carried Yun into the chamber and a scene of mass pandemonium.

A large, pancake-shaped section of the ceiling had collapsed, trapping a man beneath. His name was Jaru, and he was known for three things: the size of his nose, the fact that he could spit farther than anyone else in his unit, and his skill with a grenade launcher. Jaru was alive because he had been bending over at the moment when the roof caved in and a nearby cargo module had absorbed the initial impact. Though half-crushed, it still served to hold the slab aloft. The trooper's boots extended out into the chamber and beat a tattoo on the floor.

Orders were shouted, bodies moved through the dusty murk, and troopers grabbed hold. Two droids, both designed for heavy-duty construction work, followed the humans into position. An officer counted to three, muscles strained, eyes bulged, and hydraulics whined, but nothing happened. That's when the next set of tremors hit.

Large chunks of rock fell, a helmet shattered, and a trooper fell. He was dead before he hit the ground. Jaru moaned and continued to kick his legs. "Grab his ankles," Yun ordered, "and get ready to pull."

If Imperial troops had been taught to understand anything, it was blind obedience. The officer gave a quick series of orders, and men leaped to obey and took Jaru by the ankles.

Once the stormtroopers were in position, Yun closed his eyes, called upon the Force, and "saw" the slab rise into the air. It was a truly desperate measure, since he had never moved anything even a quarter of that size during his apprenticeship or in the years since. But he couldn't leave Jaru lying there, couldn't leave him to die, couldn't . . .

Beads of perspiration dotted the Jedi's forehead, fingernails bit into the palms of his hands, and his lips formed a grimace. Light flared beyond his eyelids, energy crackled, and something moved.

The stormtroopers cheered. Yun opened his eyes, caught a glimpse of the slab floating a meter off the ground, and suddenly lost his concentration. The rock hit the floor with an enormous thump, cracked down the center, and split into pieces.

Yun, certain that Jaru had been killed, felt a horrible sense of despair. That's when the officer slapped him on the back, Jaru materialized between a couple of troopers, and the whole thing was over.

They loaded Jaru onto a makeshift stretcher and carried him toward the surface. The rest of the work party followed. The tremors were gone now, and it was then, while he followed the officer up some well-worn steps, that Yun realized what he'd done.

"Yes," Rahn confirmed. "When the chips were down, you forgot about the dark side — yet the power you needed was there. Think about it."

Yun *did* think about it. Long into the night. There were dreams, but none focused on death, and a smile found his lips.

The administrative deck was only a few levels above the surface. That made it easier for the ground troops to come and go. The office was rather Spartan and likely to remain that way. Unpacked boxes were stacked against an unfinished wall, an unfinished cable run dangled through an access panel, and the air smelled of sealer.

Sariss regarded Yun across the top of her somewhat cluttered desk. He looked the same but *felt* different, although the nature of the change escaped her. She had heard about the rock-raising incident, everyone had,

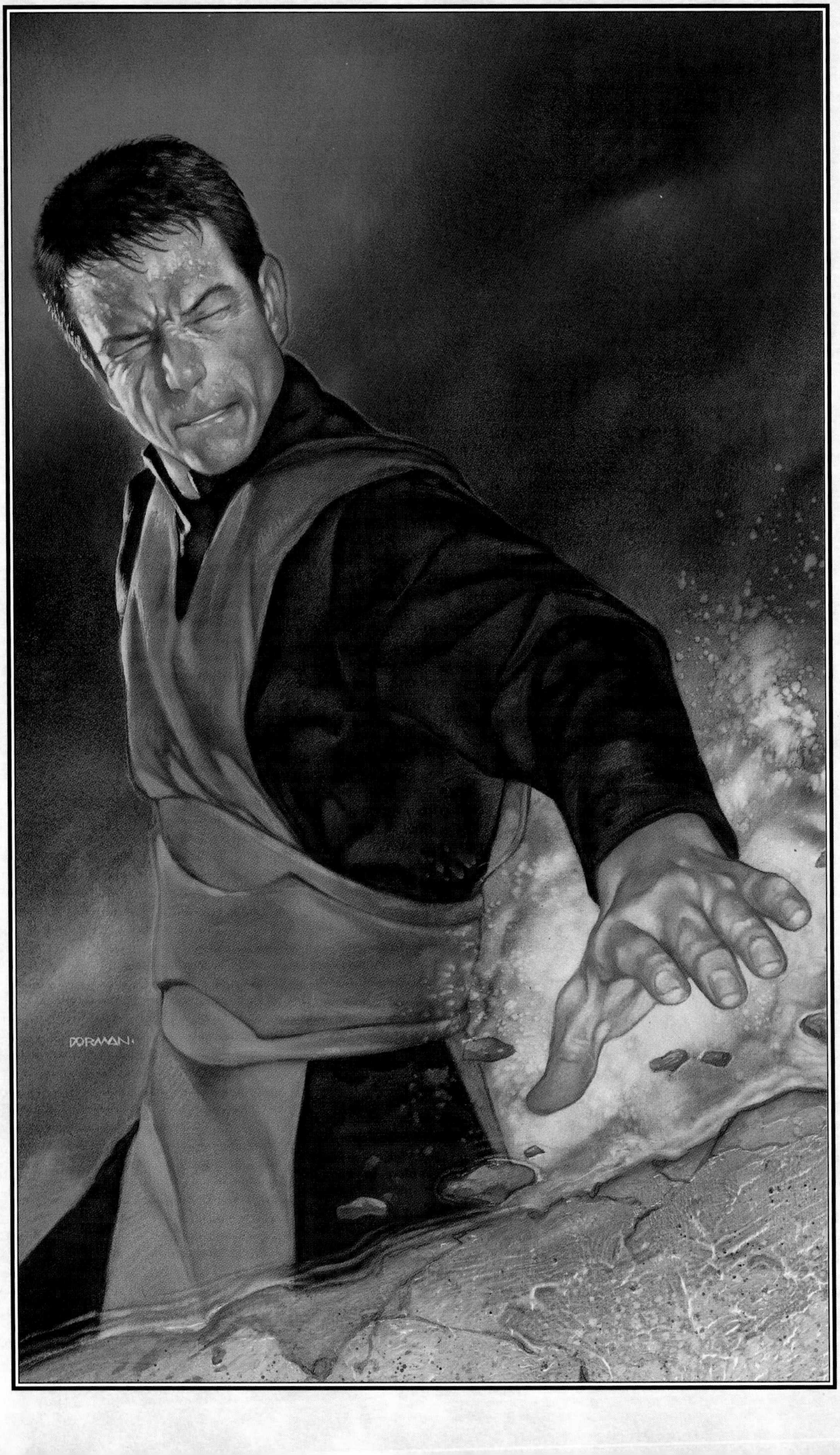
DORMAN

and read the officer's report. Even Yun admitted that the whole thing had been an anomaly, a near miracle that he wouldn't be able to replicate. The episode *still* pointed to an extremely strong talent, however, one that might prove superior to her own one day, a possibility that had never crossed her mind before. Perhaps that was it — perhaps Yun had gained additional confidence and was starting to show it. A not-altogether-pleasant possibility within a highly competitive meritocracy. Sariss summoned a smile and forced it onto her lips. "You've done well . . . even Jerec agrees."

Yun looked pleased. "Thank you."

Sariss chuckled. "Better wait till you hear what I'm about to say — you could change your mind."

Yun raised an eyebrow. "A new assignment? Something worse than herding screamers around? It hardly seems possible."

"Oh, but it is," Sariss assured him cheerfully. "It seems that a patrol," she glanced at her data pad, "Zulu, Able, Mary 341 to be exact, is forty-two hours overdue."

"Comm contact?"

"None."

"Aerial search?"

"Four aircraft, low altitude, standard pattern. No luck."

"Probe droids?"

"Dispatched . . . but nothing so far."

Yun was silent for a moment. "Why me?"

Sariss shrugged. "Why not? The sun will do you good. Besides, this requires some brains. An entire patrol disappeared without a trace. Why? Jerec wants to know."

"What about the screamers?"

"I'll put Boc on it."

Yun smiled. "Count me in."

Sariss grinned. "I thought you'd like that."

———

Yun could have requested a skimmer, crawler, or even an assault shuttle but had opted for an AT-ST and an AT-AT instead. Partly because the machines made excellent platforms from which to observe the surrounding countryside, partly because they had enough firepower to level anything he was likely to encounter, and partly because he liked the lumbering machines. Not just the way they looked, like slab-sided monsters, but the sense of power they conveyed. He rode in the two-man, seven-meter-tall Scout — while the larger and more heavily loaded machine brought up the rear.

The AT-ST's pilot was a second lieutenant by the name of Momo. He preferred "Mad Dog Momo" but had been unable to plant the nickname among the troops. Perhaps because of his choirboy face, a rather engaging grin, and the fact that he had never fired a shot in anger. Momo brought the walker up out of the ravine and onto the hard-packed plain. He looked at the control panel and over to the Jedi. "This is it, sir — the eastern boundary of their patrol area."

Yun nodded. "Take a break, lieutenant. I'm going up top."

"Sir! Yes, sir!"

A servo whined, the top hatch folded open, and Yun climbed the bulkhead-mounted rungs. It was hot outside, especially after the air-conditioned interior, and he squinted into the light. The Jedi emerged just in time to see the AT-AT lurch to a stop and pause a respectful distance away. The monster's head swiveled as its pilot used the chin-mounted sensors to probe the surrounding rocks.

Yun removed the electrobinoculars from the pouch on his belt, turned his back to the transport, and looked toward the north. He didn't see any tracks, nor was he likely to, since the patrol had been mounted on a skimmer plus two speeder bikes. He lowered his glasses. So what to do? The authorized patrol area had been searched from the air — and now on the ground. If the vehicles — or the remains of the vehicles — were visible, someone would have seen them by now.

So what about the areas *outside* of Lieutenant Aagon's authorized patrol area? Where would they have gone, and why? Yun had a theory about that — a theory based on his tour of the missing men's quarters. Every single one of Aagon's troopers had trophies hanging over their bunks. Sphere-shaped organisms with large, light-gathering eyes and delicate-looking tentacles.

No one seemed to know where the trophies came from or how the stormtroopers happened to acquire them, but Yun could guess. It was boring out on patrol, and Aagon, a resourceful type by all accounts, had discovered a way to liven things up. In doing so, he had routinely left the area he was assigned to patrol and gone where? South into the badlands? West toward the tower and his superior officers? East toward the saw-toothed mountain range? No, none seemed very likely, not given the nice smooth hardpan that stretched to the north and natives who were rumored to roam it.

His decision made, Yun returned the electrobinoculars to their pouch, descended the ladder, and issued a new set of orders. The walkers turned toward the north, increased their rate of speed, and continued the hunt.

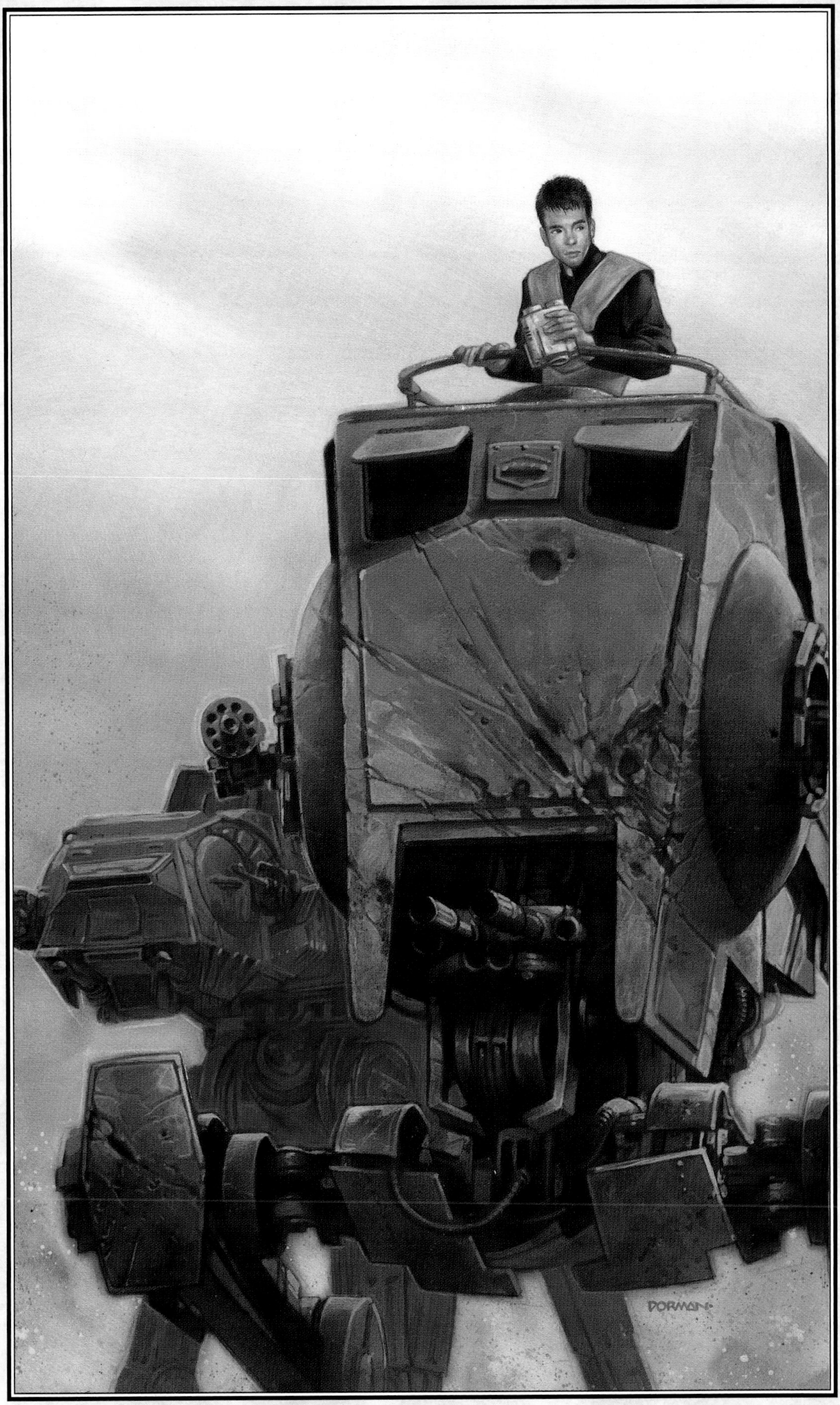
DORMAN

Kyle marveled at how pretty Jan was. Her eyes were closed, so that the long, dark lashes came close to touching her cheeks, one of which was smudged with dirt. One hand rested on her blaster, the other lay palm up, seemingly defenseless. He knew better, of course — and was careful not to touch her. "Hey, Jan — time to wake up."

"Wha?" Jan opened her eyes, blinked, and rubbed them with her fists. She looked at her wrist chrono. "What's the deal? I thought we agreed to sleep in for a change?"

"A nice thought," Kyle agreed, "except that Fido spotted an Imperial patrol. An AT-ST and an AT-AT — both headed north."

Jan rolled out from under the covers, grabbed her pants, and pulled them on. Kyle grinned, and she stuck out her tongue. "Lecher."

"Only for you . . . "

"Good," Jan said, buckling the blaster rig around her waist, "because I'd sure hate to fill out a whole bunch of reports explaining your untimely death."

Kyle tried to look terrified and followed her out of the one-time armory and into the main part of the temple. Grif Grawley was waiting. "The skimmer's ready . . . let's go."

Kyle nodded. "You think they're headed here? That we'll have to lead them away?"

Grif shrugged. "Hard to say. I hope not . . . but better that than to have them find both the temple and the *Crow*."

"How 'bout Floater? Should we bring him along?"

The colonist shook his head. "Naw, the daylight is too hard on him. Besides, Floater ain't built for this kinda thing."

The agents agreed, followed the colonist to the recently liberated skimmer, and took off. It was afternoon, so the occasional butte cast long, dark shadows toward the east. Grawley made use of them whenever he could, darting from one to the next, doing everything he could to maintain a low profile.

Finally, after fifteen minutes or so, the colonist dropped the skimmer into a dry riverbed and followed it toward a dramatic-looking mesa. "There's a good hiding place near the base," he explained, "and a trail to the top. We'll have a good view from there and, assuming they stay on the same course, plenty of time to react, if necessary."

Jan was tempted to ask what options they'd have if Imperials *didn't* maintain their present course but managed to hold her tongue.

True to his word, Grif guided the landspeeder into a semicircle of rocks, shut down the engines, and grabbed his pack. The agents did likewise. None of them planned to stay — but it paid to be careful.

Much of the trail was natural, following as it did an ancient fault line where the forces of sun, wind, and rain had carved the softer material away to reveal the underlying sedimentary rock. Still, there was no escaping the fact that intelligent, tool-using beings had improved on what nature started by cutting ledges into otherwise sheer cliffs, demolishing dangerous overhangs, and creating turnouts when the path grew narrow. Who were these mysterious engineers? Like so much about Ruusan, there was no way to know.

It took the better part of a half hour to reach the top — and Kyle was out of breath. Grif, by contrast, seemed entirely unaffected — a fact the younger man found annoying. "Come on," the colonist urged, "let's head for the east side. We oughta be able to see them by now. I sent Fido home, so he won't be spotted."

The surface of the mesa was flat and littered with loose rock and a few hardy plants. The remains of broken-down walls marked the outline of an ancient fortress. One of these ran fairly close to the edge, and Grif motioned for the agents to take cover behind it. They obeyed, produced their electrobinoculars, and peered toward the east. The sun was just about to set, but Kyle had no difficulty recognizing the boulder and the smaller rocks that attended it. This was the place where the battle had been fought and the dead lay buried.

"Look!" Jan said, pointing to the southeast.

Kyle turned, saw something blur through the viewfinder, and brought the device back. There was no mistaking the walkers or their destination. Kyle lowered his glasses. What had attracted them to this particular location? Chance? Or something more? Whatever it was, he didn't like it. What if the Imperials found something? Security was tight as it was — additional precautions could make an already difficult mission nearly impossible. He met Jan's gaze, knew what she was thinking, and shrugged his shoulders. "Time will tell, Jan . . . time will tell."

———※◆※———

The walkers came to a halt just south of the rock pile. The AT-ST stood guard while the massive AT-AT knelt to disgorge a pair of crawlers and a company of stormtroopers. Corporal Niko Smith cleared the ramp, sprinted for some cover, and fell on his belly. His sergeant, a grizzled veteran named Zonka, glanced over his shoulder, saw who it was, and nodded. "Gee, Sarge, it seems like we've scrambled over every boulder, rock, and pebble between here and the tower. What's the deal?"

"About a hundred credits a week and the Empire's heartfelt gratitude," Zonka replied. "Now get your butt in gear."

Smith grinned, waved his fire team forward, and scrambled over the rocks.

Yun opened the top hatch and watched while the troops fanned out, advanced by squad, and entered the jumble of stone. It was just another pile of rock to them — a chore to be dealt with as quickly and efficiently as possible.

Not to him, though. No, this place was different somehow. A battle had been fought here . . . and people had died. But when? A week ago? A thousand years? There was no way to be sure.

The sun dropped below the mesa off to his left. It looked blacker than black against a backdrop of gloriously pink light. And there was something else, too, a nearly undetectable fluctuation in the Force, the kind that signaled one or more intelligent minds.

Not too surprising, since some of the colonists had survived the attack on Fort Nowhere, except that Yun *knew* at least one of the minds, or thought he did.

The man in question was an Imperial renegade, the son of the very Rebel leader who had discovered the Valley of the Jedi and subsequently been executed. He was a Jedi who had been considerably weaker then, but still strong enough to fight Yun to a standstill and then spare his life. An act which the Dark Jedi had found puzzling — and initially interpreted as a sign of weakness.

The discovery sent thoughts whirling through Yun's mind. A Rebel Jedi, here on Ruusan — why? To stop Jerec, of course, to free the imprisoned spirits, to counter all that Yun had dedicated himself to. It was an amazing discovery, and the Jedi had just started to think about it when Lieutenant Momo tugged on his pant leg. Yun descended into the cockpit. "Yes?"

"Sorry to bother you, sir, but the ground pounders found something."

"What?"

"A helmet, sir, with RW957 written on the inside."

Yun checked his datapad. Trooper RW957 had been a member of the missing patrol all right — which seemed to confirm his thesis: The patrol crossed out of its assigned area, ran into some opposition, and lost the subsequent fight. That, combined with the fact that the Rebels had one or more agents on the ground, led to an obvious conclusion. A conclusion that Yun decided to keep to himself.

"It's getting dark. Pull back the troops, establish a defensive perimeter, and hold for morning. We'll complete the search then."

Momo nodded. "Sir! Yes, sir!"

Yun climbed up through the hatch and stared out toward the mesa. The other mind was there, all right — still watching, still waiting. Yun considered his options and was surprised to discover that he had some.

The obvious course was to report everything he knew, attempt to capture the Rebels, and acquire more status. More status, more respect, and more opportunities to kill people. And what of the screamers? The whole process of thinking about them as personalities, of empathizing with their plight, had changed the way he felt about them. Jerec planned to keep them in confinement — to use their power for his own dark ends. And what about the uncounted billions upon whom his heavy hand would fall?

Yun knew that he lacked the courage to champion their cause directly — but what if there was another way? What if all he had to do was ignore something that might or might not be true? Besides, a debt was involved, and debts must be paid.

The Jedi made his decision as darkness cloaked the land. He formed the thought, not for the other man, but for himself. "You spared my life . . . and I'm sparing yours. Use the gift wisely."

⟫•◦•⟪

Kyle lowered his electrobinoculars and put them away. "So?" Jan inquired. "What do you think?"

The other agent shrugged. "I can't be certain . . . but I think they have a Jedi with them . . . and he knows we're here."

Jan looked alarmed. "Then where are the TIE fighters? How come we're alive?"

Kyle shook his head. "I have no idea."

"So we go in?"

"That's what we came for."

"Yeah," Jan said thoughtfully. "That's what we came for."

The first of three moons popped over the eastern horizon and threw light across the land.

CHAPTER 5

The Rebels put the *Crow* down about five klicks from the target. It was dark, and the maneuver called for some fancy flying. The kind Jan had perfected over the last few years. It was a long way from the Valley — but as close as they dared come. The area was crawling with troops, attack droids, and AT-STs. By landing in a canyon, and covering the ship with camouflage netting, they hoped to escape detection.

Wee Gee beeped forlornly when ordered to remain behind, but Kyle was adamant. The droid would be a liability when it came to mountain climbing — and they had enough problems already.

The scouting party consisted of Kyle, Jan, Grif, and the bouncer called Floater.

Once the ship was secured, they set off in what Kyle knew to be a southerly direction. Floater led them through a labyrinth of twisting, turning canyons. How the bouncer managed to navigate through the maze was a mystery.

Kyle was surprised by the ease with which the native managed the mountainous terrain. Especially given the extent to which his species had adapted to life in the open desert. The seemingly fragile, balloon-like body and tentacle-style arms were deceiving though. Thanks to his negligible body weight and multiple limbs, Floater climbed with ease. And, while the humans were forced to rappel down the face of vertical cliffs, the bouncer loved to fling himself out into the void and float to the ground.

The darkness made the trek even more treacherous, and if it hadn't been for their night-vision goggles, the humans would have been unable to proceed.

All went well, *very* well, until the Rebels were half a klick from the Valley. Dawn saw the group ascending the nearly vertical slope of a brittle ravine. Floater had the lead, and Grif came next with Kyle and Jan strung out on ropes below.

Grif had just scrambled up onto a broad shelf when he heard the unmistakeable sound of jets firing. An attack droid, now alerted to the Rebel's presence, rose from a dark cleft in the ledge to Grif's left, who did the first thing that came to mind — he charged.

The attack droid had two sometimes countervailing objectives: to gather intelligence and kill intruders. The second imperative took momentary precedence over the first. That being the case, the machine met charge with charge.

There was no time to pull his blaster, so Grif opened his arms and swore as the machine slammed into his body.

Kyle heard a noise and looked up just in time to see the attack droid, Grif plastered across the front of its casing, sail out over the abyss. It would have been comical if the droid hadn't seized one of the colonist's legs and crushed it with a pair of powerful pincers.

Grif roared in pain, pulled his half-meter-long hunting knife, and rammed it through the robot's thin alloy skin. The blade, which had been fashioned from diamond-hard hull metal, sliced through the machine's wiring harness and shorted the guidance system.

Jan locked herself in place and waited for a shot. The droid spun on its axis and took Grif for a ride. Jan wanted to fire but was afraid to do so. The odds of hitting Grif were way too high — not to mention the fact that her rope had started to sway.

The outposter was furious now, stabbing the machine over and over, and screaming his hatred. "This is for Katie, this is for Carole, and this is for me!" The settler hit something critical, and the attack droid staggered and then accelerated away. There was a momentary flash of light as it hit the canyon wall and fell to the rocks below.

Kyle felt Grif's death via the Force, and Jan bit her lip.

But there was nothing they could do — nothing but turn back or go on. Kyle scrambled onto the ledge and waited for Jan to join him.

Common sense argued that they go back — but the importance of the mission urged him on. They were close, *so* close, and there was no assurance that conditions would improve later. In fact, it seemed logical to suppose that the Imperials would tighten their grip, making any sort of incursion that much more difficult. Still, there were other lives at stake, and Kyle had no right to make decisions for Jan or Floater.

Kyle waited until Jan was on the ledge and held a brief council of war. "There's no way to know if the droid sent some sort of report, but we

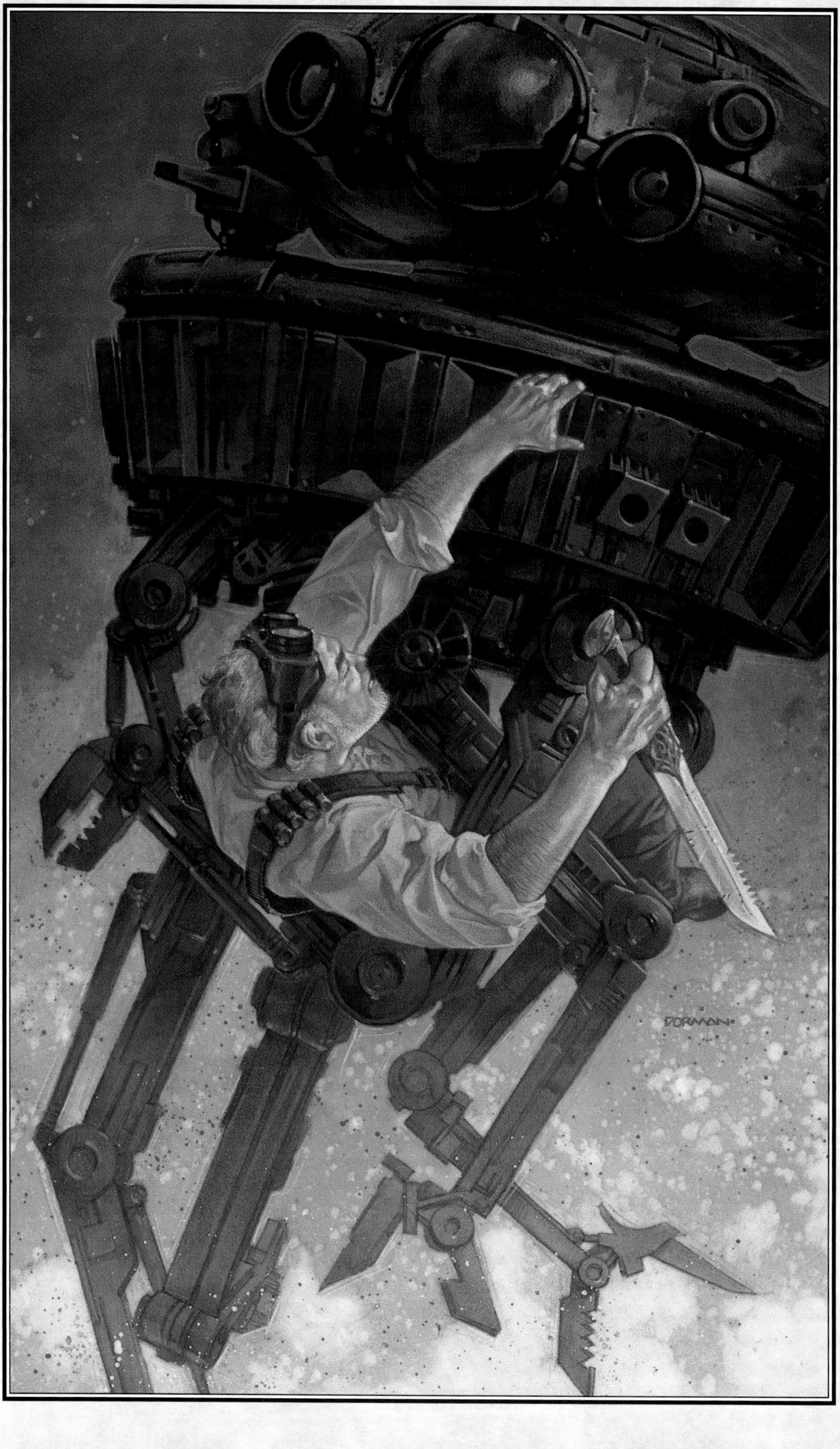
DORMAN

should assume it did. The Imperials will send out a patrol — and it will find the wreckage."

"*And* Grif's body," Jan said soberly.

"And Grif's body," Kyle agreed. "But what will they conclude when they find it? That he was part of a group? Looking to penetrate the Valley? Or a loner who wound up in the wrong place at the wrong time?"

"We can hope for the second possibility," Jan said judiciously, "but the first seems more likely. Smart people would leave in a hurry."

Kyle scanned her face. "And?"

She shrugged. "We have a mission to carry out. Let's get on with it."

Kyle nodded, looked for Floater, and couldn't find him. He pulled the night-vision goggles down over his eyes and tried again. The native was high above — still climbing. The Rebel grinned and pointed upward. "Well, if actions speak louder than words, then we know what Floater thinks . . . Let's go."

The next few hours were difficult, because of both the physical demands involved and the constant threat of discovery. A shuttle rumbled over their heads on one occasion — and a speeder-bike-mounted patrol passed through an intersecting arroyo on another. The Imperials were *so* thick, in fact, that Kyle was about to look for a hiding place when Floater led them to the aqueduct. It was about ten meters across and six high. Unlike the open irrigation canals common on many planets, the aqueduct incorporated a lid designed to limit the amount of water lost through evaporation. A lid that hid the Rebels from ships passing above.

The fact that the ancient waterway followed the contour of the land and led toward the Valley of the Jedi made it perfect. Kyle gave Floater an approving pat and followed the native into the darkness.

—➤◆◄—

Jerec stood, hands clasped behind his back, and stared out through the transparisteel window. Or that's the way it appeared, given that the Jedi was blind. However, "seeing" involves as many dimensions as "knowing," and Jerec saw many things that were hidden from others, not the least of which was the metaphysical storm that raged around the Valley below and the power imprisoned there.

The thought brought a smile to Jerec's lips. The Valley was everything he had hoped for and more . . . By tapping the power resident there and shaping it to his will, the Dark Jedi would control the Empire. No, not the pathetic remains of what Palpatine and others had frittered away, but something new, something glorious, something never seen before.

An Empire that reached *beyond* the accomplishments of the past,

95

beyond the surrounding star systems, *beyond* neighboring galaxies to include all that was or would ever be — now that was a goal! *That* was an empire.

He would have to be careful, however, *very* careful, since the forces that prevented the Jedi spirits from leaving the Valley had weakened with the passage of time and needed to be strengthened. An escape would be disastrous, since the power he required flowed from the prisoners. No need to worry, though, since repairs had begun and would soon be complete. The thought pleased him, and the Jedi frowned as a voice sounded from behind him. "Lord Jerec?"

"Yes? What now?"

The officer, a relatively junior lieutenant, swallowed nervously. "A report, sir . . . from Attack Droid AD-43. A party of three humans and an unclassified alien passed through Perimeter Two and are headed this way."

"Current status?"

"We aren't sure. AD-43 was destroyed. Other assets have been dispatched but haven't arrived yet."

The Jedi considered the officer's words. Now that the Valley was under his control, Jerec was in no particular hurry. He needed time to prepare, but more than that, time in which to savor that which destiny had placed before him, much as a gourmet might linger over a rare and carefully prepared dessert.

There was leakage, though — leakage that could double or even triple his ability — and whet his appetite for more. The Jedi Master directed a thought outward, steered a circle around the cauldron of churning energy, and located a place where a steady stream of pitch-black energy had broken through the protective shell and strobed into space.

Jerec chose a single shaft of negative energy, drew on its power, and felt himself expand. Bigger and bigger until his mind was everywhere, until he was one with the dark inner fabric of the Force itself, until he stood on the very brink of what he perceived as being all-powerful.

Not the state of enlightenment that so many prattled on about, but a state in which power could be accessed, shaped, and applied — all without the years of tedious meditation, study, and apprenticeship that proponents of the light side considered so necessary. Even better was the *next* step, the step *beyond* Jedi Mastery, into which Jerec now passed.

And it was there, in a state approaching all-knowingness, that he swept the ethers for signs of life. Thousands appeared, each instantly identifiable, each distinct from all the rest. He felt the lieutenant, only meters away, frightened and eager to leave; his bodyguards, their minds blank with boredom; Sariss, seething with plans; Boc, relishing someone else's discomfort; Yun, confused and unsure; Maw, looking to express his rage; animals, following the dictates of their genetic programming; and there, closer than he would have thought, the intruders. And not just *any* intruders — but *Kyle Katarn*!

But wait — the boy had changed, had grown into more than an annoyance: a Jedi Knight! Not entirely unexpected, since Jerec had been aware of the boy's potential before he had, but surprising nonetheless. A self-taught Jedi was nearly unheard of — unless! — and the truth flooded his mind. The youth had a mentor: Rahn!

Laughter came as if from a long way off — and Jerec felt a sudden stab of fear. He felt a desire to reach out, to crush that which opposed him, but brought the impulse under control. It was an interesting development, but not an immediate threat.

"Besides," Jerec mused, directing the thought outward, "even the best blade can be turned against those who forged it."

The laughter stopped, and a smile touched Jerec's lips. A nerve had been struck. Somewhere within the maze of beliefs, thoughts, and experiences that made up Kyle Katarn's personality, a flaw existed, a flaw that, like Yun's need for approval or Boc's senseless sadism, could be leveraged. The thought pleased the Jedi, and a decision was reached. "Maintain surveillance. Keep me informed."

The lieutenant's boots made a clicking sound as he popped to attention. "Sir! Yes, sir!"

A column of troops wound past the tower and made their way toward the ancient storerooms hidden within the Valley's walls. The harvest continued. Life was good.

⇒►◦◄⇐

The aqueduct was old, *very* old, or so it felt as Jan followed Kyle toward a distant pinpoint of light. Their glow rods projected blobs of light onto walls smoothed by the passage of water. Side tunnels appeared from time to time, their mouths gaping open, hinting at destinations deep within the rock.

Kyle said, "Watch your step," but not before something crackled underfoot. Jan directed her light downward. The skeleton, or what remained of a skeleton, belonged to a species she hadn't seen before. Had it been sentient? The eye sockets looked reproachful — as if the answer was obvious.

The light grew brighter, and the tunnel opened onto a ledge. Floater gestured with his tentacles, and Kyle crawled out. Jan followed. A wall of hand-fitted stone provided some cover, or so it seemed until a pair of TIE fighters roared by, banked around a pillar of rock, and disappeared.

Jan low-crawled to Kyle's side, got up onto her knees, and looked over the side. A tower soared hundreds of feet into the air. Landing platforms sprouted to either side, as did retractable loading arms. Jan watched as a heavily laden freighter broke contact, dropped fifty meters, caught itself, and lumbered away.

The ship would have to wend its way through a series of interconnecting canyons before emerging over the desert where it could build speed. Speed that would allow it to break free of the planet's gravity well and pass through the atmosphere. A sure sign that the Imperials had found something worth stealing. There were other freighters, too, along with shuttles and a gaggle of TIE fighters.

Kyle scanned the valley below. He watched a pair of AT-STs lumber along a trail, a trio of attack droids scoot toward the tower, and a column of stormtroopers march toward a prefab building. Jan nudged his arm. "So, what do you think?"

"It's worse than I imagined," Kyle responded, scanning the column through his electrobinoculars. "*Much* worse. The Imperials really have their hooks into this place."

Jan nodded. "That's for sure."

"Wait a minute," Kyle said softly. "Look who's here."

The Jedi handed the electrobinoculars to Jan and pointed toward the tower. "On the topmost landing platform. A man and a woman."

Jan focused on the very top of the tower and allowed the glasses to drift downward until a platform appeared. The woman wore black, as did the man. "I see them — who are they?"

"The man is Jerec," Kyle answered thoughtfully. "The woman is one of the many Jedi who serve him."

"Like the ones you killed on Sulon?"

"Exactly."

"So what do we do now?"

"You wait here," Kyle said, "while I visit the tower."

"I'm coming, too."

"And leave Floater all by himself?"

Jan regarded the Jedi with open suspicion. Was he trying to protect her? While using the bouncer as an excuse? Or was he genuinely concerned for the alien's safety? It was impossible to tell. "You'll get into trouble."

Kyle grinned. "And you'll get me out."

Neither noticed the sky-eye that rode the thermals above them — nor were they aware of the high-res holo beamed to the tower.

The hours after Kyle's departure passed with excruciating slowness. The sun rose, the temperature increased, and Floater was forced to retreat into the relative darkness of the aqueduct. Jan, fearful that she might miss something, remained where she was.

It was difficult, however — difficult to remain hidden, and difficult to stay awake. It had been a long, strenuous night, and that, combined with the warmth of the sun, made her drowsy. That's why the combat skimmer was able to get so close and Jan turned too late.

The skimmer, the stormtroopers, and the knowledge that she had committed a terrible error all registered on Jan's consciousness at the same moment.

The vehicle carried a half-dozen troops. An officer pointed and yelled.

Once alerted, the Rebel was fast, *extremely* fast, and the blaster seemed to leap into her fist. She fired, the officer fell out of the skimmer, and the pintle-mounted energy cannon burped in response. The beam passed over Jan's head and hit the aqueduct.

Super-heated rock exploded in every direction, and the opening collapsed. An officer yelled, "Alive, you idiot!" and Jan fell backward as the skimmer threatened to crush her. It took less than three minutes for the troopers to pile out of the skimmer, pat down the agent, and secure her hands.

An officer, anonymous behind his visor, gave the necessary orders. "Put her aboard . . . shift enough rock to make a hole. There could be more — and I want every single one of them."

Jan remembered the side tunnels that led deep into the mountain-side and knew where Floater would go. It was a small consolation — but better than nothing. Her thoughts turned to Kyle. What would he do without her? And if it came to that, what would she do without him?

———o———

Kyle felt something was wrong but couldn't put a finger on what it was. He pushed his consciousness outward, searching for danger, and found nothing but tranquility. Comforting — but impossible given the circumstances. It was as if someone or something had smothered his senses. But that was impossible, wasn't it?

The uneasiness continued as Kyle lowered himself down through a three-sided chimney and dropped to the ground. He'd been lucky, almost *too* lucky, but there was nothing he could do about it.

The Jedi considered the rope and decided to leave it. Assuming that his luck held and he made it back, the line would come in handy.

The passage of time, combined with natural forces of erosion, had

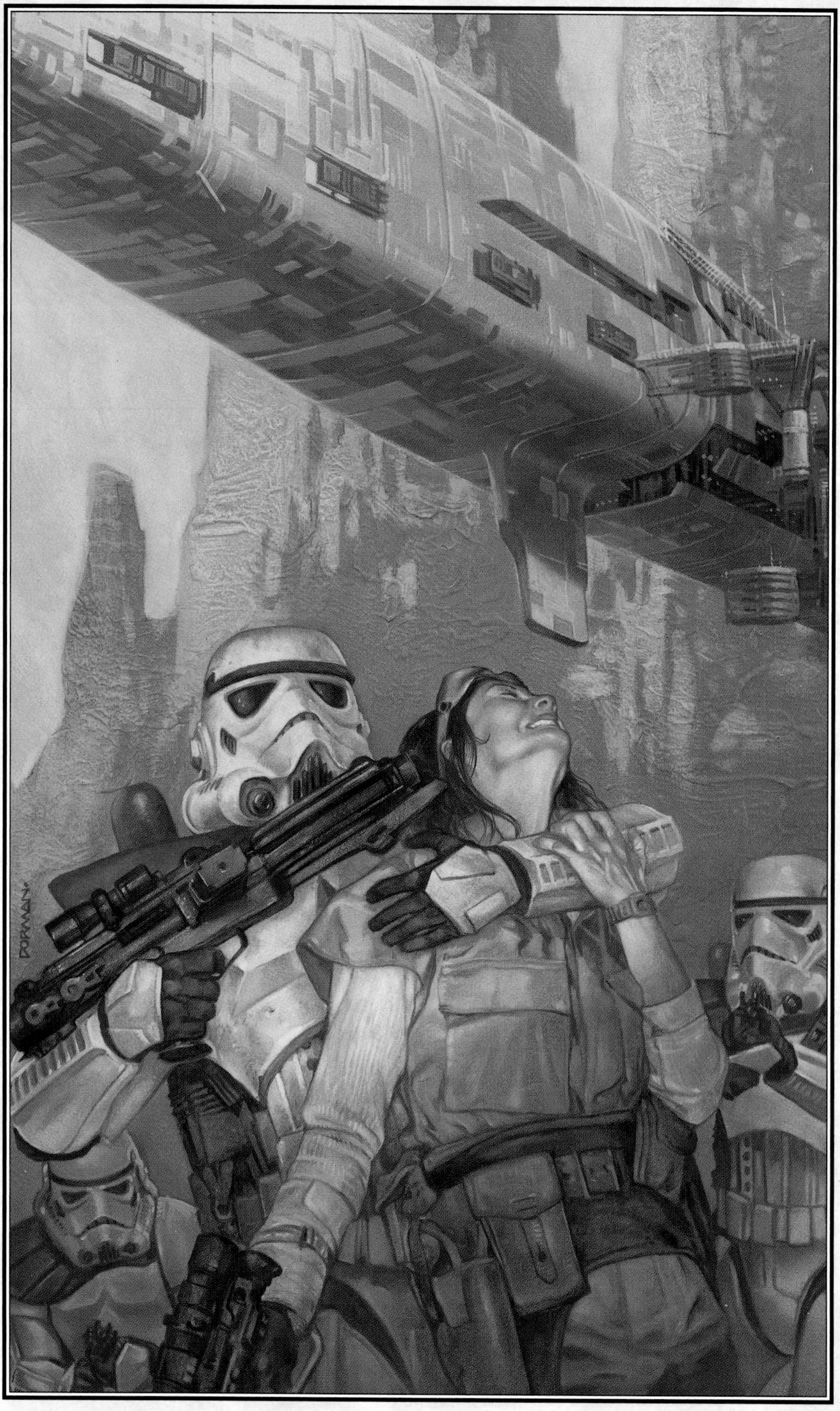

caused boulders to accumulate at the foot of the cliff. The Rebel used them to conceal his movements.

The tower made an excellent and highly visible landmark. The agent waited until he was opposite the structure, worked his way out toward the Valley floor, and peeked through a gap in the rocks.

The area between Kyle's hiding place and the base of the tower was completely open. To cross was out of the question. All he could do was wait.

An hour passed. The sun pounded down, sweat poured off his body, and his water disappeared one swallow at a time. The agent's situation was desperate by the time a tractor appeared and offered the only chance he was likely to get. He saw a single guard sitting next to the driver, engaged in conversation.

Kyle waited for the tractor to draw abreast of his position, dashed across the intervening space, and jumped onto a coupler. A train of fifteen cars jerked along behind the tractor and raised an enormous cloud of reddish brown dust. It made him cough, but the noise generated by the tractor's engine covered the sound.

The train passed a half-filled vehicle park and wound past the tower. Kyle waited till the moment was right, jumped to the ground, and made a dash for one of the enormous footings on which the vertical structure rested. He waited for an alarm. None came.

Kyle turned and scuttled toward the tower's inner core. The sentries, their attention focused on the Valley beyond, stood with their backs to him. The Rebel marched by, hit the "up" button, and waited for the lift. The doors opened and a brace of Commandos appeared.

Kyle had his lightsaber tucked under his arm, much as an officer might carry a swagger stick, and nodded as he marched by. The Rebel did a smart about-face, saw that one of the Imperials looked as if he wanted to say something, and frowned.

That, plus the lightsaber, did the trick. The Dark Jedi, because that's who the Imperials assumed he was, were notoriously short-tempered. So much so that neither one cared to try his patience.

The door rolled into place, and the turbolift rose with what would have been commendable speed had Kyle been in a hurry. Yes, he was Jedi, and yes, he had proven himself against three of the Dark Master's subordinates, but the thought of going one-on-one with Jerec himself terrified him. What he needed was help — a whole bunch of it.

Thought was answered with thought as Rahn flooded Kyle's mind. "The Force is with you — as am I."

Kyle forced a grin. "What? No breaks?"

"Not lately," the Jedi Master replied dryly, "not since your arrival on Ruusan."

"Good — I need your help."

"Knowing that, and admitting it, signals strength. The half-man awaits. Use my name to seize the advantage."

Who was the half-man? And what difference would Rahn's name make? Kyle wanted to ask a half-dozen questions, but the lift started to slow. The agent readied the lightsaber, allowed his thumb to rest on the switch, and kept his eyes on the door.

The lift came to a halt. A tone sounded, and a light came on. The door rolled open, and a messenger droid scurried through the opening. It squeaked, sent a signal to the turbolift, and waited for the platform to fall.

Kyle approached the entrance, looked out onto an empty platform, and heard machinery whir. The message was clear: get off or take his chances on the lift. There was no sign of a half-man, whole man, or any other kind of man.

Surprised by Rahn's error, and more than a little apprehensive, the Rebel stepped out onto the platform. The tone sounded, and the door closed behind him. A loading ramp jutted off to the right, and a cargo ship hung beyond that.

Kyle took two steps forward, felt something "pop," and felt a sudden flood of sensation. Nothing exotic, not by his standards anyway, just the sort of input he normally received via the Force but had been unable to access for the last ten to fifteen minutes. Why?

The answer came with terrifying speed. Something, he wasn't sure what, hit his shoulder and sent him sprawling. He rolled onto his back, jumped to his feet, and lit the lightsaber. The air crackled and filled with the odor of ozone.

That was the moment when Kyle realized that Rahn had been right — the lower half of his opponent's body *was* missing! It was the Force that held him up off the ground. The Dark Jedi's skull was shaved and seemed too small for his body. Hatred filled his eyes and pulled at his thick-lipped mouth. Two equally enormous arms hung from his muscle-bound torso, and one ended in a lightsaber.

In addition to holding the Jedi up off the deck, the Force exerted its influence over other objects as well, including nuts, bolts, pebbles, a ration bar, and various bits of wire. All of which orbited the half-man's body as if he were the sun and they were his planets. The lightsaber buzzed with malevolent energy, and his words had a grating sound. "I am Maw . . . prepare to die!"

"Maybe," Kyle replied calmly, "remembering that my friend Rahn already cut you down to size."

The effect was electrifying. Maw's face turned purple with anger, and

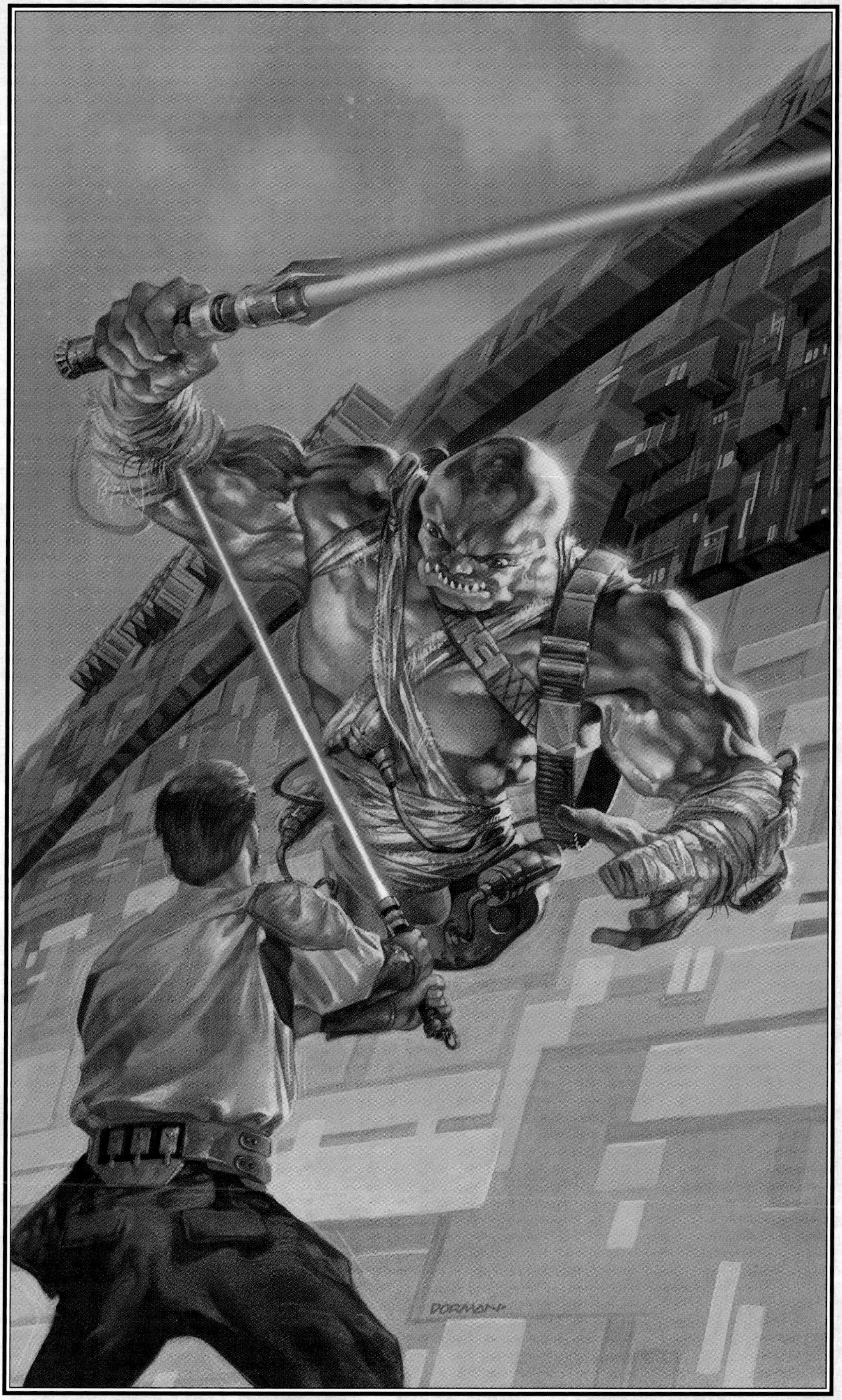
DORMAN

he uttered a roar of pure, undiluted rage. He accelerated with far greater speed than Kyle had anticipated. The Rebel fell backward, allowed the Dark Jedi to pass over him, and slashed upward.

Maw bellowed with pain, lost his concentration, and hit the deck. The lightsaber sailed out of his hand, and debris rained onto his head and shoulders.

Kyle took a single step forward, eyed his opponent's back, but couldn't bring himself to do it. Maw supported himself with his fists, turned, and looked upward. "I'm defenseless . . . kill me! Or do you lack the courage? As your father did before you?"

Kyle dropped his head. Anger, contained and controlled for so long, flowered within. He felt it radiate outward, seep through his body, and tingle at his fingertips. The lightsaber hummed, and his fingers wrapped and rewrapped themselves around the well-worn grip. Here was one of the people who had murdered his father — and not *just* his father, but hundreds, maybe thousands, more. Killing such a person would be just, yet . . .

Maw grinned demonically. "Your father was on his knees, whimpering like a child, as Jerec struck him down. I placed his head on the spike where the rest of the Rebel scum could see it."

The lightsaber blurred as it rose and fell. The blade entered the half-man's left shoulder, sliced through his chest, and exited through the right side of his body. There was an explosion of blood as Maw fell into two distinct pieces — and Kyle felt energy swirl around him. *Dark* energy, attracted by the nature of his act, ready for use.

Shocked by what he had done and sickened by the slaughter, Kyle backed away. A voice came from behind. "Excellent . . . The journey to the dark side has begun. But there is more . . ."

Kyle turned to discover that Jerec, Sariss, and Boc had stepped off the turbolift, and that Jan was with them. Boc gave Jan a wholly unnecessary shove. She stumbled and caught herself. Kyle saw the bruises on her face and realized that her arms were bound. Jan forced a grin. "Sorry, Kyle, looks like I can't bail you out of this one."

Jerec gave her a push and Jan fell. He pointed to where she lay. "Strike her down! Realize your *true* destiny . . . your *true* power."

Time stretched thin. Jerec felt Kyle's hunger, the ambition that seeped up through his consciousness, and allowed himself a smile. *Here* was the flaw that Rahn feared, *here* was the lever he'd been looking for, and *here* was a hunger that matched his own.

Jan watched the other agent's eyes, saw temptation flicker there, and wondered if she had misjudged him.

Boc simpered, did a little dance, and waited for someone to die. He wore two lightsabers, one thrust through the back of his sash and one in front.

Kyle looked from Jerec to Jan and back again. The fact that he'd been tempted, *could* be tempted, made his stomach churn. "No."

The Dark Jedi drew upon the energy that leaked out of the Valley, gave it shape, and hurled the construct at Kyle's chest. The blast threw the Rebel backward onto the loading ramp. He staggered and had just managed to reestablish his footing when a second, more powerful explosion hurled him back into the cargo ship.

The lock sensed his presence, and the hatch started to close. The ramp disintegrated. The ship tilted away, and fell toward the rocks below.

Jan rose, tried to make her way to the edge of the platform, and was slammed to the deck. Boc laughed and put a foot on her chest.

Unaware of what was going on above, Kyle smashed into a bulkhead and knew what he had to do. Head for the belly of the ship and pass through the docking port. It was his only chance.

The docking port? Why the docking port? But there was no answer — just an overriding sense of urgency.

The inner hatch opened, and Kyle ducked through and found himself in one of two corridors that ran the length of the ship. As with most ships of her design, there was an emergency drop shaft that ran top to bottom through the ship's hull. Kyle staggered as the nose tilted down. He dropped to his knees and opened the access door set flush with the deck.

A ladder was welded to one side of the drop shaft. The Rebel clamped the side rails between his boots, slid downward, and triggered the hatch. The agent dropped through and landed on the docking port. Or would have, had the freighter been level. Because the ship was tilted nose down, the Rebel hit *forward* of the hatch and had to battle his way up.

Precious seconds passed while he cycled through the lock and entered a familiar-looking compartment. The *Crow!* The Imperials had located the ship and flown it to the tower. The agent heard a beeping sound and knew that Wee Gee was locked in one of the storage compartments. There was no time to free him, however. *If* he could bring the engines on-line . . . *if* he could break the connection . . .

The odds were against him — but there was little else that Kyle could do. He fought his way into the cockpit, dropped into the pilot's position, and hit the emergency bypass switch. Alarms sounded and lights flashed as the vessel's nav computer took exception to the breach in protocol. Freed from normal safety procedures and responding to the Rebel's prayers, the engines came to life.

Kyle bit his lip, hit the emergency release button, and felt the vessels part company. The application of power, plus a turn to port, increased the distance between them. The agent pulled back on the control yoke, saw a flash as the cargo ship corkscrewed into the ground, and fought for altitude.

The *Crow* shook violently, rattled Kyle's teeth, and slammed into a rocky spire. The port engine sheared off, the nose dropped, and the ground rushed up to meet her. The hull hit, bounced, and started to slide.

Kyle thought about the safety harness, wished he was buckled in, and felt his head strike the control panel. The Rebel was unconscious by the time the ship skidded to a halt. The dream, if it was a dream, seemed incredibly real.

Rahn smiled as if welcoming Kyle home. He wore a cream-colored robe with a hood that fell in folds across his shoulders. "That which *is* flows from that which *was*. The best way to learn is to *feel* what it was like."

The Jedi faded from view, and Kyle became aware that another mind coexisted with his. Though seemingly unaware of *him*, he was aware of *it*, and all that it contained. There were memories of a youth spent exploring the stars, a passion for a woman long dead, and a planet frosted with ice and snow. There was a weariness as well, for the mind was very, very old.

But evil cares little for age or infirmity. It grows where it can, sinking its roots deep into the rich fertilizer of ego, lust, greed, envy, and hatred, sending new shoots to the surface where they form a tangle from which nothing can escape. That's why Tal had taken his lightsaber down from its place above the hearth — and joined the Army of Light. "Tal? Are you awake?"

It wasn't until the Jedi opened his eyes that Kyle realized they'd been closed. A man sat across from him: a giant of a man with shoulder-length blond hair, a lantern-shaped jaw, and ice-blue eyes. They twinkled merrily. "There you are — I was afraid you'd sleep through the surrender."

Tal chose his words with care. Hoth might be a Jedi, and a great one at that, but many voices vied for his attention. So many it was difficult for the big man to sort them out. Which was why Tal reserved his council for only the most important issues — and chose his words with care. "There won't be a surrender — not today, at any rate."

Lord Hoth's face grew dark as if hidden from the sun. "You try my patience, old one. We conjured an army from nothing . . . We turned freighters into warships . . . We traveled through many systems, conquered all that the dark ones placed in our way, and arrived on Ruusan. Here we fought seven terrible battles . . . Battles in which thousands of Jedi died. *In spite* of their superior numbers, *in spite* of their brutality, *in spite* of their willingness to invoke the dark side of the Force, the Brotherhood of Darkness lost all but two of those engagements. Only one choice remains to them . . . and that's surrender. Why deny the obvious?"

Tal shrugged. "Because what we consider to be unthinkable they will accomplish in a heartbeat."

"What?" Hoth demanded. "What do you fear? Put a name to it. I cannot act on a single being's forebodings . . . no matter how trusted that individual may be."

Tal searched for the words that would explain his misgivings and came up empty. "I'm sorry, sire . . . it's a feeling. Nothing less and nothing more."

Hoth shook his head irritably. "I'm surrounded by every sort of sycophant, soothsayer, and clairvoyant. A pox on the lot of you . . . Come, it's time to go."

Tal used the arms of the campaign chair to push himself up and out of the seat. He bowed. "I pray that I am wrong, sire, for nothing would please me more. I will be at your side no matter the outcome."

Hoth smiled and took the old man's hand. "I know and take strength from it. Come . . . history awaits."

The Jedi leader collected his lightsaber, threw his cape back over a shoulder, and strode into the sunshine. The Army of Light saw him emerge, and a thousand voices roared his name.

Tal took one last look around the inside of the tent, knew he would never see it again, and hobbled toward the entrance.

It took the better part of the morning to pull the troops together, march up the winding road, and enter the Valley. Tal was thankful for the fact that the going was slow, since age had robbed his once-responsive body of its strength and quickness.

But not his mind. If anything, it was stronger, anchored by more than eighty years of experience and alert to the slightest stirring of the Force. Tal could *feel* what the Dark Ones had achieved. The Force seemed to congeal like blood in a wound, to thicken the air around them, to press against their chests.

The others felt it, too, for they were Jedi and wise in the ways of the Force. Expressions turned grim, muscles strained against the invisible burden, and the air crackled with unreleased energy.

Poles appeared along both sides of the road. Each bore the scavenger-pecked remains of a Jedi — their clothes filled with momentary life as the wind pushed in to explore them.

Cliffs crowded the road and served as vantage points from which the

Dark Ones could watch. Their ranks were thinner now, *much* thinner, but no less intimidating. Their banners flapped languidly in the breeze, their eyes projected hate, and their hands rested on well-worn weapons. For these were the survivors, the beings so skilled at mental-physical combat that seven hard-fought battles had not only failed to bring them down but served to hone their skills. Tal knew that they were — and would always be — dangerous.

A double row of heads appeared, one to each side of the road, many still recognizable. Tal saw one of his students, her eyes empty of the humor for which she'd been known, and felt a deep sense of sorrow. He thought about Hoth, about begging the Jedi Master to call the whole thing off, but knew it was useless. The same determination that made Hoth a great leader would result in his downfall. Nothing could turn him . . . nothing but death itself.

The chambers, almost as large as the ego they had been created for, stretched for miles. Their location deep within the ground had proven to be bomb proof, missile proof, and assault proof. Up till now, that is. More than a thousand battle-torn flags hung from the walls — many of which still bore the blood of those who had carried them.

The leaders to whom the flags had been entrusted, or what remained of those leaders, were arrayed before the flags. Some were human — many were not. Their eyes were blank, their cavities were filled with preservatives, and their bodies were supported by steel rods.

The trophies stood in two inward-facing ranks and formed the letter V. Kaan sat at the point where the lines came together on a throne made of bones. He had white hair, a prominent forehead, and a finely pointed chin. Power radiated away from the Jedi like heat off a sun-baked rock. It caused the air to shimmer, sent static through pocket comms, and hurt unprotected minds. His eyes were filled with hatred and probed the beings in front of him. "They come."

Kaan's second, third, and fourth in command were dead, killed during hellacious battles of the past few weeks. Number five, the Jedi known as LaTor, stepped forward and bowed. Kyle bowed with him. "Yes, my lord. They come."

"We have no way to stop them? No strategy for salvation?"

LaTor, half his face obscured by a blood-stained bandage, shook his head. "No, my lord, none I am aware of."

"Then we must create one! Surrender is unthinkable. Assemble my Jedi."

"Yes, my lord."

It took the better part of two hours to spread the word, to bring what remained of the Brotherhood into chambers, and to settle them down.

Once assembled, the Dark Army was woefully small. Less than two thousand Jedi compared to ten times that number that had followed Kaan into the first few battles. Still, small though they were in number, these were the smartest, strongest, and most powerful of the lot, for the rest were dead, having been overpowered by Hoth and the Army of Light. The air hummed with barely controlled energy. Kaan stood and the chambers fell silent. His eyes roamed the audience, found those he knew to be leaders, and claimed their minds.

"Greetings, brethren . . . and welcome to darkness. Our great and noble cause has come to an end. The forces who favor anarchy over structure have won. For what is this 'democracy' they speak of if not the absence of order? Of reason? Surely the strong should rule — for that is nature's way.

"But we must forget what could have been — and focus on what *is*. Defeat looms only hours away and with it, the loss of all we had hoped for. I ask that you join me in one last task. The creation of a weapon so powerful that when it is detonated, the victors shall become the vanquished and be swept from the pages of history."

Kaan was a skilled orator and knew when to stop. The chambers fell silent. LaTor allowed the silence to build . . . and broke it with the traditional salute. "Kaan rules!"

The answer came like thunder and echoed off the chamber walls. "Kaan rules!"

And so the decision was made to place death before life. More than a thousand highly trained minds were focused on a single task. First came the creation of a mental construct that was analogous to a bomb casing. A container in which energy could be stored. Then came the process of turning the Force inside out, of tapping the darkness within and channeling that energy into the newly created vessel.

Time hung suspended, the air crackled with barely suppressed energy, and three of the Jedi died, their minds overcome by the violence of the process. Others went insane, rose with weapons drawn, and were executed by the master-at-arms.

Kyle was a novice compared to those around him and might have been killed if it hadn't been for LaTor and the other Jedi's strength. For LaTor was strong, *very* strong, and Kyle was impressed by the power resident in the dark side. The power and the relative ease of access . . . a temptation for anyone with the necessary talent.

Finally, their robes soaked with sweat and their hearts beating like trip hammers, the Brotherhood was done. The thought bomb was complete. The time had come to venture out into the sunlight, to embrace the victors and drag them into hell.

———⊰•◦•⊱———

The final confrontation came in the Valley located above the chambers. It was there, in an amphitheater carved by the forces of wind, rain, and erosion, that the Brotherhood of Darkness had assembled and waited for death.

And it was into the Valley that Tal dragged his aching body, knowing that death hovered nearby but determined to protect his master's back.

And it was there that Kaan, the Lord of Darkness, met Hoth, Defender of the Light, and gestured to the cliffs that rose on every side.

"Welcome, Lord Hoth. Welcome to the grave and darkness from which none will ever emerge."

The thought was relatively trivial, much as the pressure exerted by a marksman represents only a fraction of his total strength but has the capacity to destroy that which he could never create.

The explosion that followed was anything but trivial, however, for it shattered the construct made to contain it and filled the Valley with destruction. Tal reeled under the impact, felt his body snatched away, and was thrown toward the stars. Joy filled his heart. Freedom! He was free from pain . . . free from . . .

Nature abhors a vacuum, however, and the emptiness at the heart of the explosion had to be filled with something, so it sucked Tal in. Tal and all the rest. Understanding filled the Jedi's mind. His screams were nearly lost among the others. "No! Please! No!"

But the matter was settled. For every action there is an equal and opposite reaction, and consistent with that law, both armies were pulled back in. A state of equilibrium was achieved as force matched force, and they were trapped. Thrown together for eternity . . . or until something disrupted the existing balance.

Tal, and his alter ego, Kyle, were still in the process of absorbing that, of understanding it, when the Rebel awoke.

110

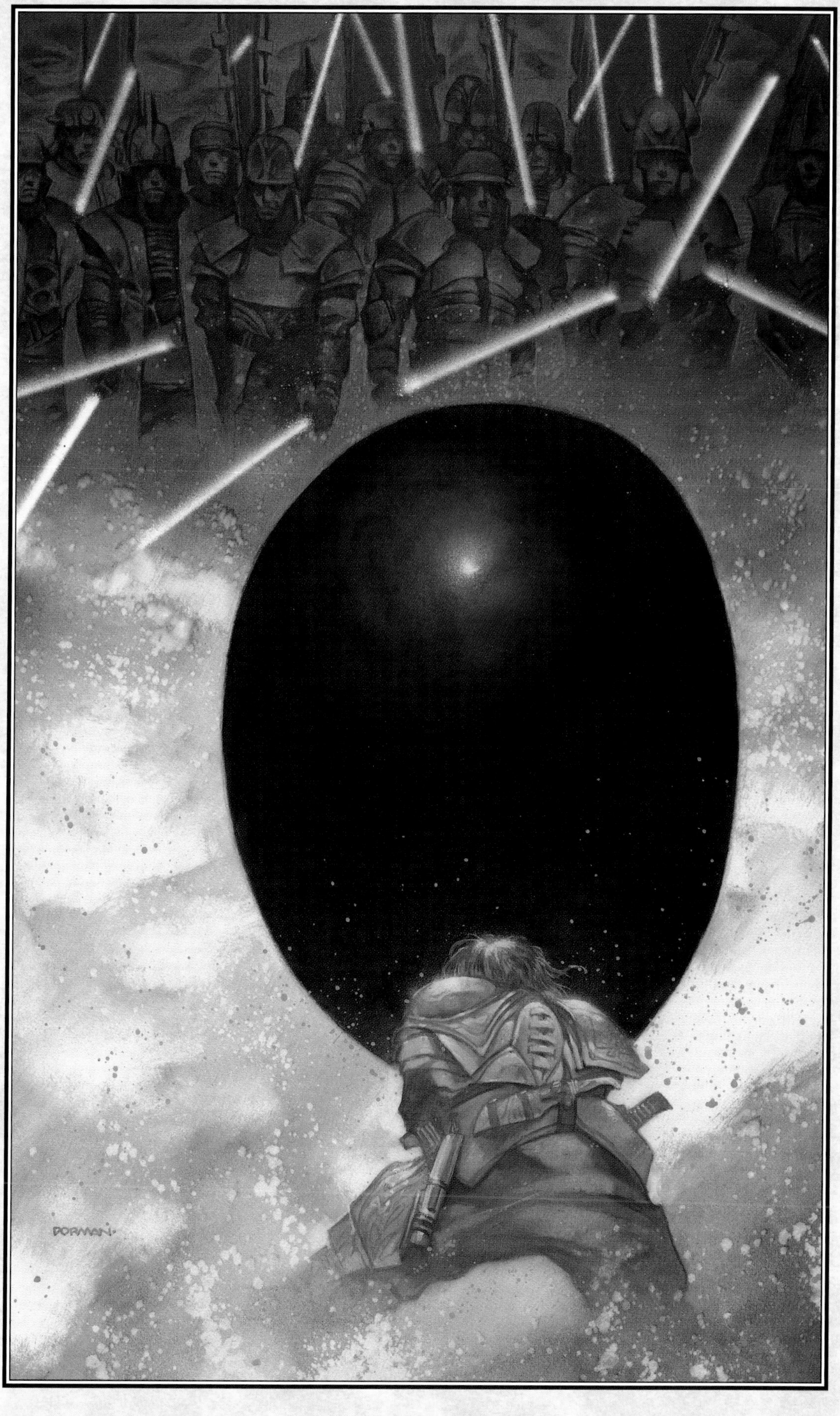

CHAPTER 6

Kyle awoke to pain, more pain than he had ever felt before and more pain than he wanted to feel again. So much pain that it took a moment to realize that it belonged to *him* — and not his alter ego, Tal.

The Rebel opened his eyes, saw stars twinkling high above, and felt cold night air enter his lungs. He tried to sit. What felt like a six-centimeter-long needle passed through his skull and entered his brain. He groaned and leaned on an elbow.

That's when Boc shuffled forward — and Kyle realized that others were present. His heart sank. The Imperials had entered the *Crow* and dragged him clear. The worm-head? It didn't matter. The female was present, her mouth pressed into a hard straight line, as was the Jedi Kyle had battled on Sulon and subsequently spared. The same one who had located the missing patrol? Yes, the personality felt the same. Their eyes met, held, and broke as Boc brought a lightsaber out from under his cloak.

"My, my . . . such a nasty crash . . . You're lucky to be alive . . . or are you? Oh, what's this? A lightsaber — no, not just *any* lightsaber, but *your* lightsaber, and a pretty piece of work it is."

Boc placed the weapon on a flat piece of shale, grabbed a rock, and raised it over his head.

Kyle tried to rise, made it to one knee, and paused as pain filled his head.

Boc grinned. "Yes? Did you want something? No? Well, let's see how sturdy this saber really is . . ."

So saying, the alien Jedi brought the rock down with all his strength. There was a crunching sound, and pieces of saber flew in every direction.

Boc chuckled. "Blast! They just don't make 'em like they used to . . . Oh well, it's not as if you built the weapon yourself. That would take brains."

Sariss drew her weapon and flicked the switch. The air popped and sizzled. "Enough . . . Tell Jerec that we located Katarn and put him down."

Boc glanced from Sariss to Kyle and placed a hand over his mouth. "Oops! That doesn't sound very promising, does it? But what did you expect? Milk and cookies?"

The Jedi broke into peals of laughter, turned, and shuffled away. Sariss turned toward Kyle and raised her weapon.

Kyle looked into the glow and thought about Jan. Was she dead? Would they be together?

Sariss tightened her grip and brought the weapon down.

Yun saw everything in slow motion, felt himself respond, and wondered why. Had he made a decision? There was no memory of one . . . Not a single decision, anyway, just a long chain of seemingly minor decisions, which, taken together, added up to an important decision. The lightsaber seemed to ignite on its own. *If* his aim was good, *if* the training paid off, he would nick his mentor's arm. She would miss — and Katarn would be spared. Not for long, probably — but he couldn't control that.

Blood flew as energy sliced through flesh. Startled by the attack, and reacting instinctively, Sariss turned. Her lightsaber rose, fell, and sliced through Yun's shoulder. The younger Jedi looked surprised, gave a gasp of pain, and sank to his knees.

Sariss was horrified. Yun, her best student and the closest thing she had to a friend, was dying. Why? It was impossible, yet there he was, kneeling before her. She screamed for a medic, and the echoes seemed to mock her. Yun's head came up. His eyes saw through her. "Sariss, can you see the light? How bright it is?" Then he was gone. He leaned forward until his forehead touched the ground and then fell on his side.

Kyle saw Sariss turn her back in his direction, saw Yun drop the lightsaber, and used the Force to "grab" it. The weapon made a slapping sound as it hit the palm of his hand. The Rebel pushed up through the pain, fought a wave of dizziness, and thumbed the unfamiliar switch.

Each lightsaber was as unique as the sentient who built it — and Yun's was no exception. It came equipped with what Kyle's fencing instructor would have called a "modified pistol grip" — meaning that carefully cast projections echoed the human hand and gave his index finger a place to rest.

Not only that, but the grip was made from a highly malleable "live" polymer that explored Kyle's hand and morphed into a solid, highly customized grip. Kyle had never dreamed of such a thing but immediately fell in love with it.

The Rebel raised the weapon into the traditional "on-guard" position and could almost hear the Academy's fencing instructor. He had a squeaky, high-pitched voice: "Keep your head up, look at your opponent, and check your balance. The point should be at eye level — or slightly lower — like so . . ." A steel blade differs from a lightsaber, of course . . . but many of the same techniques apply.

Sariss turned. Her eyes burned with anger. There was more than enough time. No cut would be fatal in and of itself, but each added to all the rest would result in a painful death. Then, after his life force had been released and his blood had mingled with the sand, she would take his head. Not that it would compensate for the pain in her arm or the ache in her heart.

Kyle swallowed, knowing his opponent was more experienced than he, and then suddenly reeled under the impact of a mental attack. This battle would be fought on *two* planes. One mental, the other physical — just like the ones in his "dream."

The Jedi accessed the knowledge gained from the long-dead Tal, blocked the mental strike and answered with an attack of his own. He launched a head cut from the third position, flexed his wrist, and extended his arm.

Though a good deal lighter than its metal counterpart, the Jedi energy weapon possessed similar characteristics. It could penetrate like a rapier and cut like a saber. A *double-edged* saber.

Sariss blocked the mental blow, wondered where Katarn had garnered such knowledge, and found herself under attack. Her opponent's skill was a surprise — and reminded her that this was no ordinary Rebel.

There were various ways to defend against his attack. Sariss chose parry five followed by a well-practiced riposte. Her blade passed under Katarn's, buzzed as it passed through the outer corona of the field created by his blade, and lunged toward his chest.

Energy crackled and popped as the agent intercepted her blow — and disengaged.

The attack had failed, so Kyle selected another. The point-thrust was a relatively simple evolution. He dropped the point of his saber, extended his arm, and lunged.

Sariss saw it coming, blocked the other Jedi's blade, and spotted an error. Katarn's wrist was too low, a little below the shoulder, opening the Rebel to a head cut. She lunged as he pulled back, saw a thin red line appear on his right cheek, and felt a sense of satisfaction. The upstart had been lucky — but she would literally cut him down to size. Yun would be revenged.

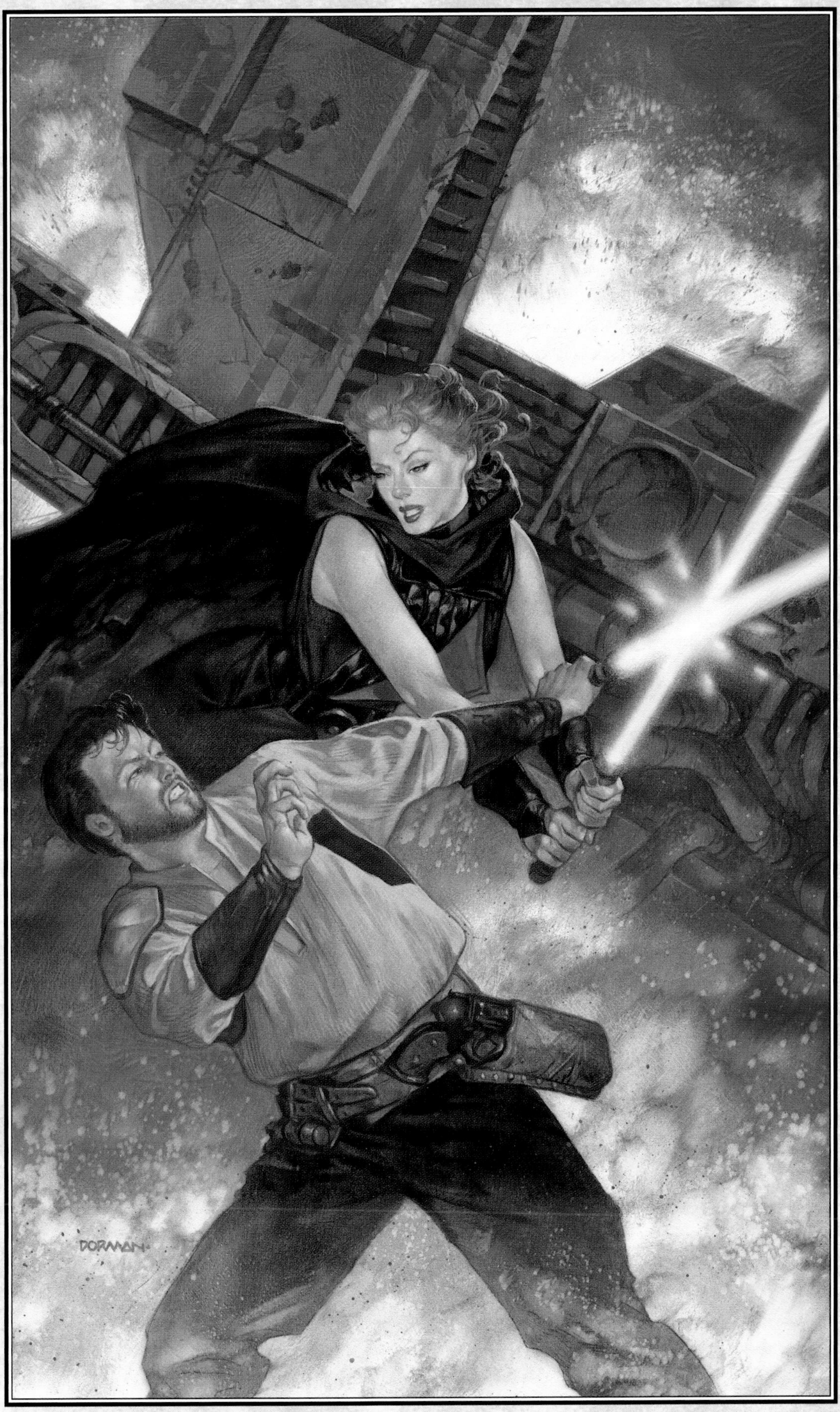
DORMAN

Kyle saw a flash of color and heard the blade sizzle past his face. His nostrils were filled with the odor of burnt flesh. His own. Pain followed. Pain layered on pain. He knew the cut was a harbinger of things to come. He was tired, hurt, and less experienced. The Dark Jedi intended to wear him down. What he needed was a quick, decisive conclusion. The agent assumed the on-guard position and called upon Tal's knowledge. What would the ancient Master do if confronted with a similar situation?

Sariss sensed the other Jedi's hesitation, mistook it for fear, and launched a feint. It was directed at Kyle's belly. He fell for it, saw her pull back, and knew the lunge would follow. He managed to parry, felt resistance as her saber clashed with his, and found the answer he'd been searching for . . .

Tal had been a student of another no-less-formal school of swordsmanship that was half-physical and half-spiritual in nature. There were many evolutions, and many "cuts," but only one that "sang" with the moment.

"The Flowing Water Cut" was for use when going blade-to-blade with an opponent. Timing was everything . . . and as Sariss withdrew . . . Kyle knew that he should "expand," following with body and spirit, like water into a vessel. And there, within the calm, to cut slowly and release Sariss from her body.

Action followed thought. His blade strobed through the other Jedi's chest and the point emerged between her shoulder blades. There was very little blood since the wound was cauterized as it was made. Sariss looked surprised. Her eyes went down toward the point of entry, up toward his, and then were gone. She fell over backward, hit the ground, and skidded on loose gravel.

Kyle just stood there, swaying slightly, struggling to absorb what had occurred. He was alive, *still* alive, which both amazed and pleased him. But what next? Find Jan? Search for Jerec? Both ideas had merit, but how?

Cliffs stood hard and black off to his left, but the sun had started to rise, throwing soft pinkish light onto a pinnacle of stone. The shadow fell downward — and pointed to the Valley below.

Suddenly, and without knowing *how* he knew, Kyle knew where to go. He said good-bye to Yun, who had sacrificed his life for something he had just started to understand, and wished the Jedi well.

Gravel crunched under the agent's boots as he followed the shadow toward the opening and that which waited below. There were sentries to contend with, and a patrol on its way out into the badlands, but Kyle ignored them. A Commando saw him and stepped forward. "Halt! Who goes there?"

Kyle extended a hand. "You have seen me many times before — and are aware of my authority."

The Commando nodded. "Sorry, sir — I didn't realize it was you."

The Jedi nodded and proceeded on his way. The area around the opening had been cleared of debris. The stairs were wide enough to accommodate four men walking abreast. They were cut from solid stone and followed the curve of the wall.

The light improved as the sun rose and sent rays of light down into the chamber.

The air thickened around Kyle's shoulders, and he heard a moaning sound, as if from a multitude in pain. Alien hieroglyphics appeared on the walls — and the Jedi reached out to touch them as the stairs carried him downward.

Light gleamed off something down in the murk. It attracted the Rebel's eye and made him curious. What could it be? A piece of scrap? An artifact?

Kyle arrived on the chamber floor, made his way to the area where the reflection had appeared, and toed a pile of debris. Metal clattered as the Jedi spotted what he'd been searching for.

He knew the object by feel alone: A multi-tool, similar to the one he carried, but older. Anyone could have dropped the device — but something, he wasn't sure what, caused the Jedi to examine the object more closely. He turned toward the light and saw an engraving: "To Dad, from Kyle."

The Jedi felt a lump form in his throat as he realized that his father had made it this far and, while unable to free the spirits within, had set their rescue in motion. Assuming that *he* lived long enough to complete the mission, that is.

What had his father felt? Having come all that way? And lacking the ability to go farther? Had he been frustrated? Fearful? There was no way to know, but one thing was for sure: The knowledge that Morgan Katarn had been there, and would expect him to persevere, strengthened Kyle's resolve.

The multi-tool made a comfortable weight in Kyle's pocket as he moved forward. His senses were heightened — and a thousand impressions flooded his mind. He had originally viewed the Force in the abstract, as something outside of himself, but not any longer. Now Kyle felt at one with the Force. It surged and seethed as if only barely contained. It trickled through the pores in his skin, filled each living cell, and displaced pain and fatigue. He felt light, strong, powerful. Was that good? Or something to be feared? The half-man's death still weighed on the Jedi's conscience and caused him to question his motives.

Cautiously, because he was both unsure of himself and of what he might encounter, Kyle approached a heavily shadowed arch. He stepped through and into the Valley of the Jedi.

A thousand tombs marched across the Valley floor. Each was different, as unique as the spirit to whom it had been dedicated, and a work of art. Years, perhaps hundreds of them, had been lavished on the vast memorial.

Kyle was overwhelmed by the pure spectacle of the place. He wandered down a corridor from which narrower walkways branched to either side. He saw statues, some of which were modeled on humans while others depicted aliens, each rendered in astonishing, lifelike detail. Here, captured in stone, was the Army of Light. Who were the artisans? And what happened to them? The bouncers seemed like the most likely candidates — although there was no way to be sure.

A head appeared above all others, and Kyle walked in that direction. It was Lord Hoth, his eyes focused on something Kyle couldn't see, a hand on his lightsaber. The Jedi looked so *real*, so *powerful*, that the Rebel half-expected him to speak.

And there, just to the Jedi Master's right, stood another familiar figure. The man stood tall in spite of the years that weighed on his shoulders. He wore a long, white beard, and even though a hood concealed most of the Jedi's face, Kyle knew who it was. Still loyal, still at his master's side, Tal waited through the years.

Hoth, and the manner in which he towered over the figures around him, gave Kyle an idea. He glanced around, spotted a tomb with a flat top, and made his way over to it. A ledge ran around the structure and served as a step. Gargoyles, their eyes bulging, functioned as handholds.

Once on top, Kyle had an excellent view of the Valley. He saw a row of columns, realized someone had been tied to one of them, and knew who it was. Jan was alive!

Kyle felt his heart leap, crossed to the other side of the slab, and looked down. Another tomb stood two meters below. The top had been sculptured to resemble the Jedi within. Kyle landed on the warrior's forehead and jumped from there to the ground. The columns were clearly visible . . . and he jogged in that direction.

If the Rebel had been more deliberate and less focused on Jan, he might have noticed a statue unlike those around it. A statue that not only *appeared* to be alive — but actually was.

Boc followed Kyle with his eyes but was otherwise still. The other Jedi might have sensed his presence if it hadn't been for a carefully constructed mind shield. Katarn was alive! But that was impossible . . . wasn't it? Where was Sariss? Yun? Both questions were answered when

Boc spotted the youngest Jedi's lightsaber, a sure sign that they were dead. No great loss in Boc's opinion — but surprising nonetheless. The Rebel led a charmed life — but not for much longer.

Unaware of Boc and the nature of his thoughts, Kyle broke into the clearing. Jan saw him and grinned. "Kyle! Nice of you to drop in."

Kyle thumbed the switch on Yun's lightsaber and used the weapon to cut Jan's bonds. Kyle's words were light — but hid a deep sense of relief. "This will cost you . . ."

Jan felt the restraints fall free and rubbed her arms. "Send the bill . . . I'm ready to pay."

"And so you will," Boc said coldly, "and so you will." There was a thump as the Dark Jedi jumped down off his perch, followed by the angry buzz of clashing sabers.

Kyle held against the other Jedi's strength — and pushed with all his might. Boc smiled. His teeth looked like tombstones. "All things come to an end, Katarn — give Maw, Sariss, and Yun my best."

The words covered action, and Jan shouted a warning. "Kyle! Watch out! He has two sabers!"

The Rebel jumped backward as the second bar of energy blurred past his face. He had noticed the second weapon during the earlier confrontation and forgotten it. A stupid, possibly fatal, mistake. Kyle was afraid. Boc sensed the emotion and shuffled forward.

"Perhaps you would like to learn something before you die. The use of two blades, one to support the other, can be traced back thousands of years and was common to both our species. The invention of lightsabers has done nothing to lessen the effectiveness of this strategy — as you are about to learn."

Actually, thanks to Tal, and the old man's considerable experience, Kyle knew something about fighting with two blades, which meant he knew how dangerous such a combination could be. Not that the knowledge would help him much, given the fact that he had only one weapon at his disposal.

"One weapon only?" a voice said within his head. "What of your mind? Are you Jedi? Or something less?"

The words, and the fact that Rahn was with him, brought new hope.

Boc advanced. His lightsabers seemed to dance before him. They hummed with barely contained malice and wove intricate patterns in the air. The movements had a hypnotic quality — and Kyle struggled to resist it.

Energy sizzled as blade met blade. Kyle retreated as Boc launched a flurry of blows. The Dark Jedi grinned triumphantly, shuffled forward, and "felt" an additional threat. He spun toward Jan. The Rebel threw the rocks as hard as she could — but to no avail. The missiles exploded as

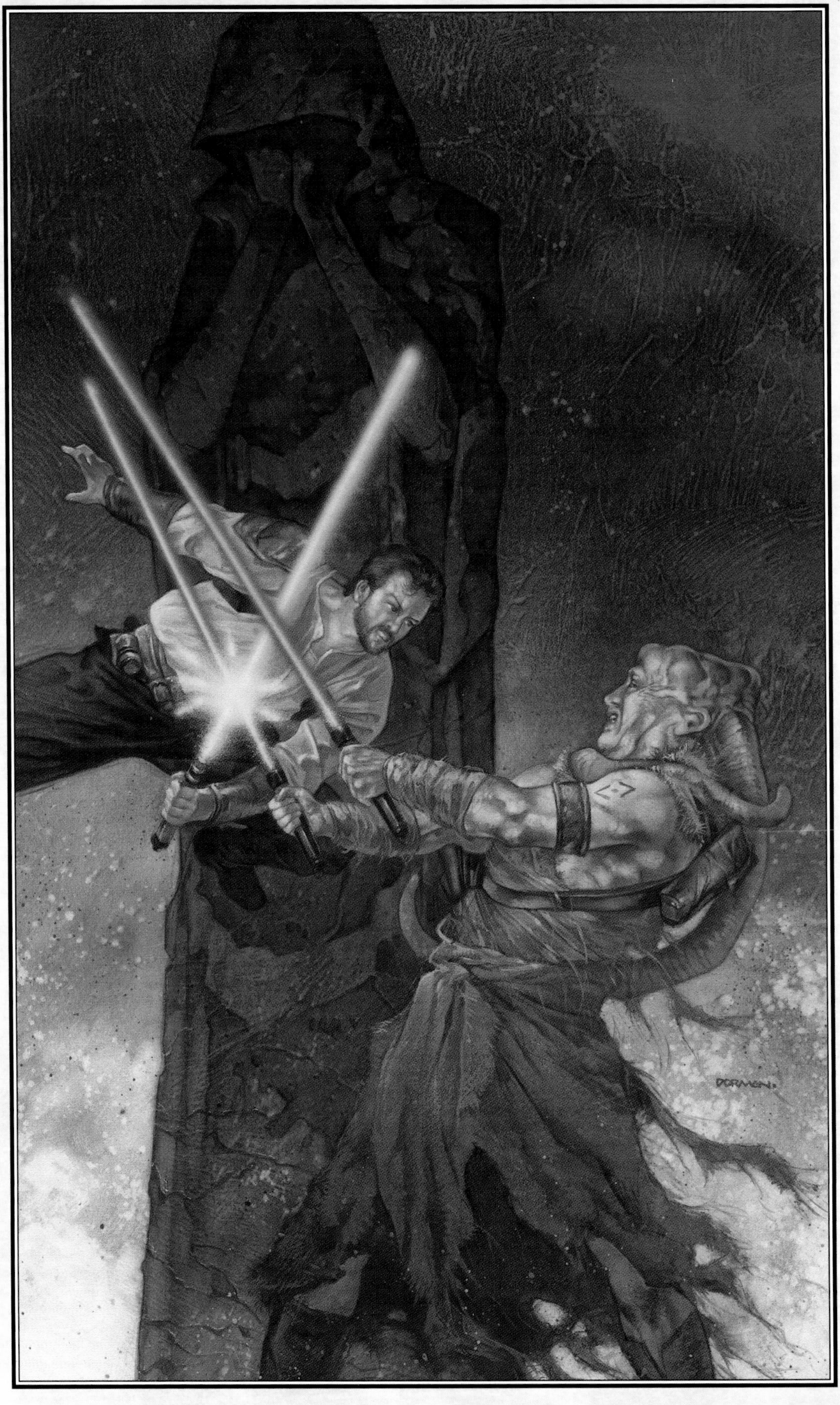
DORMAN

the sabers touched them and hurled red-hot bits of rock in every direction. Jan staggered and fell over backward as a bolt of energy hit her mind.

The rock attack hadn't inflicted any damage, but it did buy some time. Kyle took advantage of the opportunity by summoning the Force, forging a spear of midnight black, and hurling it toward his opponent's chest.

Boc staggered, dropped the lightsabers, and grabbed the invisible shaft. Kyle watched, fascinated as the other Jedi struggled to remove the weapon and failed to do so. He tripped, fell, and collapsed. A statue towered above him. Newar Forrth, one-time commander of the Third Legion of Light, appeared pleased.

The sound of distant laughter echoed through Kyle's mind. "Wonderful! That's the second time you called on the dark side. Now do you understand? The power is all around you, waiting to be used. Kill the girl, cut your ties to the past, and claim the future."

Unaware of the interchange, Jan ran into his arms. "Kyle! Are you all right? I don't know what you did — but it worked."

The Rebel wrapped his arms around her and kissed the top of her head. "Come — let's find Jerec."

"That shouldn't be too hard," Jan replied. "Look!"

Kyle looked and saw shafts of light shoot upward to play across the ceiling. They ran in that direction. Jan ducked as a screamer howled by her head. "What was that?"

"Don't worry about it," Kyle responded. "It can't hurt you."

"Can't hurt you, can't hurt you, can't hurt you," a chorus of voices echoed, only to be supplanted by a tidal wave of incomprehensible babble that closed around them.

Many of the spirits were insane, having lost track of reality during eons of imprisonment, but some were not. They offered conflicting advice.

"Refuse the dark side, boy."

"Leave us! Flee while you can!"

"Fight him, son, for there is no alternative."

There were other voices as well — some of which spoke alien tongues — but none as clear as the one from within. "To know where evil grows and permit it to flourish is to accept responsibility for all that follows."

A mound appeared in front of them. It marked the center of the Valley and the point from which the rays of light emanated.

Someone had left footprints in the soft soil, and Kyle followed them up onto the mound. Jan followed. The light, which had grown more intense, strobed upward and splashed across the rocky ceiling.

Kyle could "feel" the power gathering around him and knew time was running out. "Stop him!" a disembodied voice begged. "Stop him before he enslaves the billions we fought to defend! Even now he strengthens the bonds that hold us here! He plans to feed on us, to take our power, to use it for evil!"

Kyle started to reply but stopped when the ground started to shake and debris rained from above. It was difficult to walk, so he scrambled on all fours, determined to reach the top of the mound. The center was hollow. Dirt fell away from the edge and avalanched into the depression below.

Jan arrived at Kyle's side, looked into the mound, and was amazed by what she saw — Jerec, quivering with the power that coursed through his body, light spilling from empty eye sockets. His voice came from everywhere at once. "Yes! Join me! Share the power!"

Kyle moved forward; Jan grabbed for his arm and missed. The Jedi jumped, fell through the air, and absorbed the impact with his legs. His lightsaber sizzled as he turned it on. "Yessss," the chorus chanted, "free us that we might merge with the Force!"

Jerec chose to ignore the lightsaber *and* the spirit voices. He spoke without turning. "Your efforts are misguided. Can you hear them? Whining and sniveling? Is that what you seek to become? Another voice in a chorus of weakness?"

Jerec turned, extended his hand, and triggered an explosion. Kyle was propelled up and out of the chamber and onto the Valley floor. The impact knocked the air from his lungs. He was lying there, trying to breathe, when an icy wind swept through the Valley.

It circled slowly at first, as if gathering energy, before steadily picking up speed. Dust and other bits of debris were vacuumed up and whirled about. Voices wailed as mist billowed and the temperature continued to drop.

Kyle made it to one knee as Jerec levitated up and out of the mound. Voices moaned as large chunks of the inner mound and paving stones followed him up.

Kyle stood, heart pounding, staring upward. What could he do? Jerec had claimed the Valley's power, had already harnessed it, and would soon rule what remained of the Empire. And then what? A *new* Empire, worse than the first, and a whole lot bigger. Despair threatened to pull him down. To come so far only to have failed those who counted on him was worse than death itself.

The Rebel watched Jerec rise and marveled at the power the Dark Jedi had unleashed. Power waiting to be used, power that could defeat Jerec, that could pull him down . . .

Kyle brought himself up short. What had Jerec said? *That's the second time you called on the dark side.* What was the magic number, anyway? The repetitions beyond which one was changed? Was it three? Four? Five?

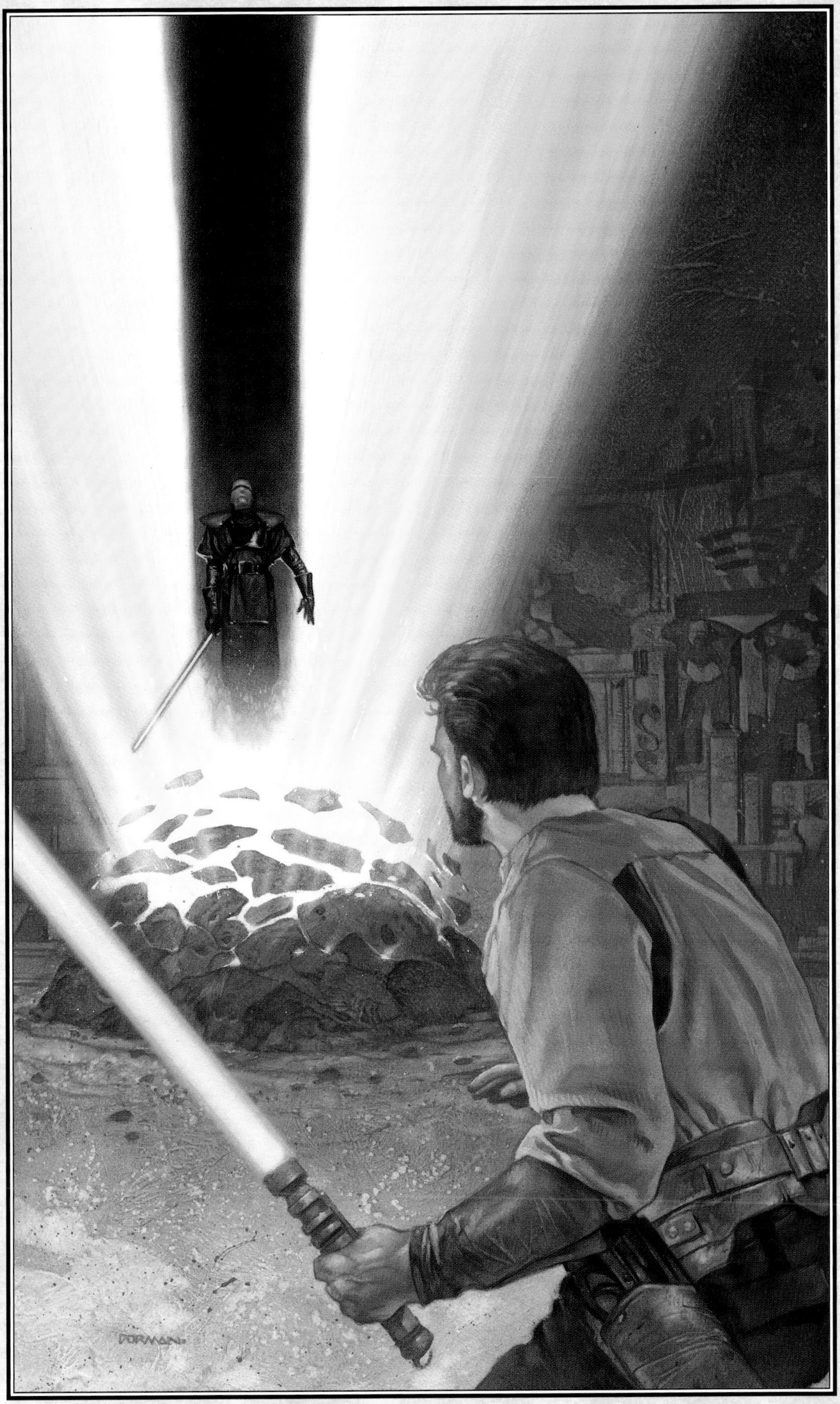
DORMAN

Suddenly, Kyle knew that the number didn't matter — that the light side offered more than enough power for any task he would be called upon to do, and that knowledge was the key.

The Jedi closed his eyes, resisted the temptation to look at the light that strobed against his eyelids, and sent a series of commands. He gathered the Force around him, shaped it into a protective cocoon, and sealed Jerec within.

Jerec felt a sense of warmth and peace as the cocoon of light formed around him. It was a wonderful sensation — and one he enjoyed, until something went wrong. The Jedi fell, struggled to stay aloft, and fell again. Something, or someone, had cut his access to the dark side of the Force . . . Who? How?

The Dark Jedi fought to break through and knew it was too late. The dark, nearly black column of energy that pushed up out of the mound had been severed, and he, along with the rocks that had risen with him, plummeted to the ground.

Kyle opened his eyes, saw the Dark Jedi fall, and knew he had taken the correct approach. By doing something positive, by *protecting* Jerec from evil, the battle had been won. The ground under Kyle's boots crunched as he approached the fallen Jerec.

Though stunned and badly bruised, Jerec was otherwise uninjured. In spite of his blindness, the Dark Jedi knew that Kyle stood over him with lightsaber in hand. His own weapon lay ten meters away — but may as well have been on the far side of the planet. Having never shown mercy to others, Jerec sought none for himself.

"Strike me down and the power of the dark side will be yours! It was I who took your father's head . . . or have you forgotten?"

Kyle looked down at the man before him and felt a strange sense of pity. Here he was, physically powerless, but still hoping to bring Kyle over or, failing that, to secure a quick and painless death.

The Rebel shook his head. "No, I haven't forgotten, and I never will." He extended his hand, felt the Dark Jedi's lightsaber strike the surface of his palm, and then threw the weapon to Jerec.

Jerec rejoiced in the agent's stupidity, leaped to his feet, and thumbed the power switch. Energy crackled as he moved forward, and Kyle came to meet him. The Rebel spun on the ball of his right foot, executed what Tal called the "falling leaf" and "slashed from the sky."

Jerec stutter-stepped, brought his weapon up and across, and waited for the inevitable result. Something warm touched his side, sliced inward, and stopped just short of his spine.

It took Jerec a moment to understand what it was, to realize that his life had come to an end, and to start his long, dark journey.

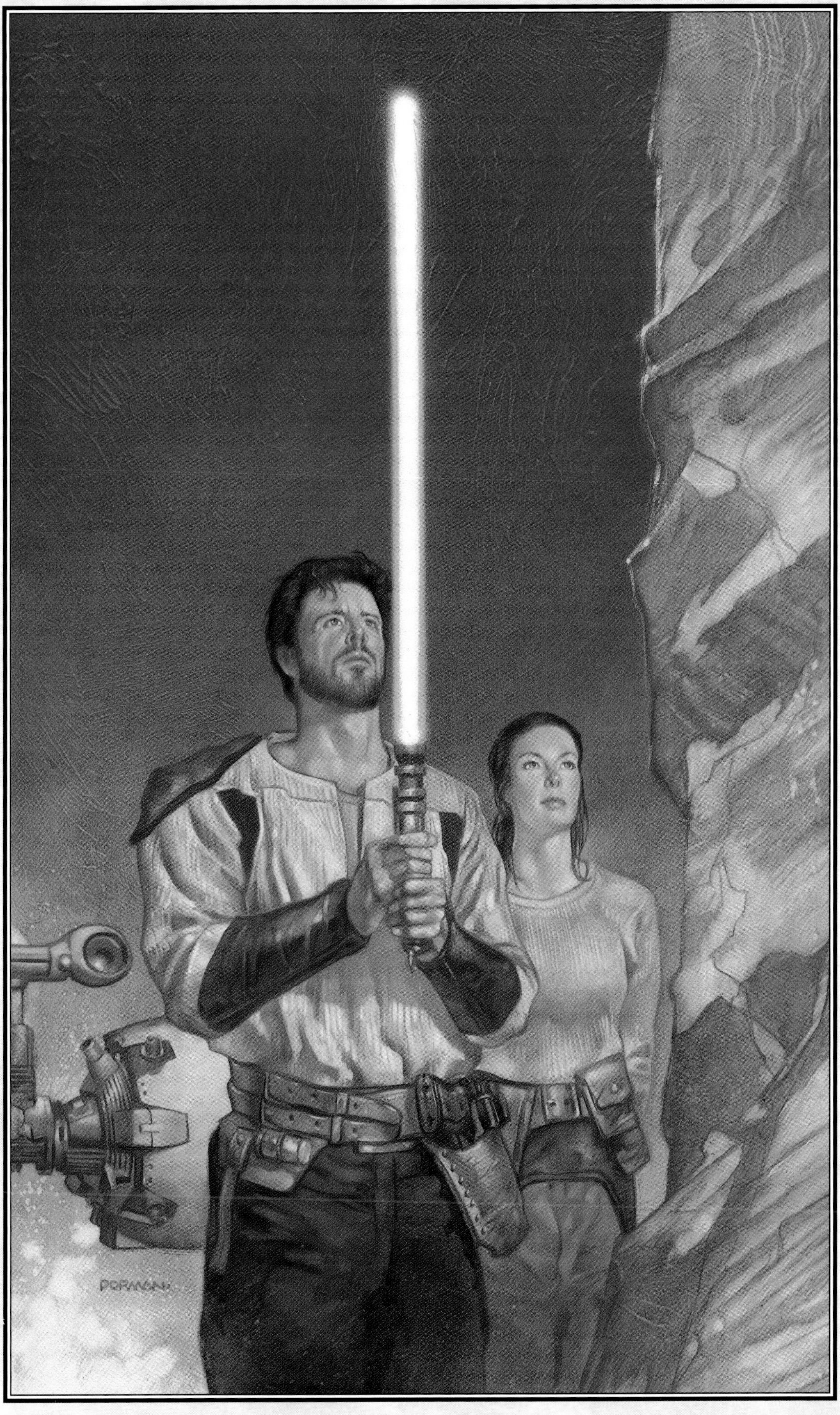
DORMAN

Jan arrived at Kyle's side as Jerec's body started to fall. It seemed to lose substance as the Force departed, and it landed like a shadow on the ground.

In the meantime, the ancient bonds that Jerec had worked so hard to repair had been strained by the recent turmoil. Now, subjected to even more stress as the prisoners hurled themselves about, the invisible fabric began to tear. One of the more active spirits spotted the hole, slipped through, and was quickly followed by another. The spell was broken! An unseen chorus screamed their joy, circled the Valley, and poured into the sky.

A joyful singing was heard as the spirits rode the wind out into the atmosphere — and Kyle felt a chill run up his spine as voices thanked him, one after another. And then they were gone. Kyle knew that the Army of Light had set forth on one last journey, that his mission was at an end.

The "storm" went on for what seemed like a long time but was no more than minutes. Finally, after the wind had died down and one last screamer had followed the rest to freedom, the Rebels turned away.

The walk out through the monuments was a slow, almost reverential affair — that ended in front of a long stone wall. Kyle whirled in response to a series of clicks, whirs, and beeps, saw Wee Gee, and grinned.

"Weeg! You survived the crash! I'm glad you found us." The droid squeaked happily and propelled itself forward.

Kyle turned toward the wall, triggered his saber, and struck a carefully aimed blow. A section of stone fell away and landed at his feet.

Wee Gee turned his vid pickup in Jan's direction, and she shrugged.

The Rebel, unaware of the byplay behind his back, knelt before the wall. He said, "Thank you, father," and Jan, who had moved close enough to see, saw two freshly carved reliefs. She had seen holos of Morgan Katarn — and knew him by sight. The other face was new, but Kyle had described him often enough, and she knew it was Rahn. There was a moment of silence as Kyle bowed his head and flowed with the Force.

Then, with Jan's hand in his and Wee Gee following behind, the Rebels made their way out of the Valley and up into the sunlight. And it was then, at that exact moment, that the prophecy came true . . . A knight had come, a battle had been fought, and the prisoners were free.